KIL

A Nov

Christopher J Harvie

For my father, John Harvie (1945-2007),
who always loved a good story

"Sainte Gertrude, garder ceux de cette nuit de la méchanceté de l'ennemi, les aider à repousser l'importune qui affligent notre pays, assurer leur sécurité et d'alerte afin que tous puissant revenir."

Author's Note

This story is a work of fiction, even though it borrows heavily from actual events.

The First World War, as encapsulated from 04 August 1914 to 11 November 1918 cost millions of lives, military and civil, and abjectly altered the lives of many millions more. Fought principally in Western Europe, the global concerns of the two power blocs engaged there opened the hostilities to Africa, The Middle East and Asia, and any stretch of water in between. Its conclusion would involve redrawing borders, and create a legacy of history which can still be felt today.

Where this story is set, on the Western Front in 1917, has allowed me a superlative event in human history to work with. My attempt to re-create this period with any hope to realism was based upon available primary documents including war diaries, reports and orders, military manuals and expert consultation. I am in the deepest gratitude to a gallery of archivists, librarians and passionate devotees to history in the work they have done in making such material so accessible.

To free myself from re-writing history, much of anything specific, all of the characters and most of the locations are made from the whole cloth of imagination. Foremost for me was to look at the war from a Canadian perspective, which could have been problematic. Canada's contribution to the war militarily was organised- our Army still is- in what is known as the "Regimental System."

Briefly, this meant that soldiers were grouped around a nucleus of command just below that of a general. From 800-1200 officers and men at different levels of strength, each of Canada's overseas regiments had their own, and quite well recorded, identity and experience of the war. I could not interfere with that.

This difficulty has been side-stepped by widening France by an arbitrary seven hundred yards, North to South, to insert the 16th Canadian Infantry Brigade, and its component units. Though I've made it appear that the 16th Bde reports to the 4th Canadian Division, an extant formation, no such Brigade numbered 16 existed. Which means of course, the one battalion within it where this story is told, The King's Own Canadian Scots Regiment, is my own creation, but founded deeply in the traditions and pride of units which would have been its contemporaries had it been real. Individuals in the same way have been given life and voice, but are by no means, least not intentional, a reflection of anyone in reality, past or present.

Above all of that, I hope you enjoy it.

Christopher J Harvie

April, 2016

Chapter I

France, April, 1917.

Snow. At this time of year, of all things. When Felix first peered out at the coming dawn, it was one of those times which his mind wished to reject, despite the evidence settling on the ground. Thick flakes, animated on a hurried breeze were collecting in drifts and in the hollows of the shattered ground. It was still too early in the pre-day half-light to tell just how badly this inopportune weather was interfering with visibility. A real problem was that if it continued to come down as heavy as this, the markers which had been surreptitiously placed in no-man's land would be obscured. Six Platoon was dependent on these landmarks to know when to change formation and direction on the advance, whose beginning was now a mere half hour away. Not only was it essential that the platoon find these cues for their own purposes, but also that they reach them at exactly the right time. The artillery fire plan, now in its final day was intricate and complex. A crowning achievement for the gunners, miles away, would be a walking barrage coordinated across the whole Corps' front. Done correctly, it would create a sheet of shellfire, moving at staged intervals ideally to protect the infantry as they advanced. Too slow, and the barrage would out distance them, negating its effectiveness. If they were too quick, the risk of falling under the very thing covering their movement was almost assured. Pacing and visual references would be life or death, there being nothing to be done to alter or stop the artillery's programme. Despite the weather, the men were warm enough, crowded in a narrow tunnel forward from the firing trench. While they had been preparing for this day, over weeks of training and rehearsals, the engineers had pushed saps well out into the land between trench lines. The sappers had spared nothing in the effort, the entire length shored up with timber gotten from God-knows-where, side galleries for dressing stations, the whole thing intricately wired for electric light and telephones. Those two things alone made this jumping off point more modern than many men could claim for the homes they had left behind in Canada. The rough-hewn walls glistened with a mix of ground seepage and the breath of almost forty men. Without was the snow, among the bursts from the tail end of the week-long bombardment-iron rain-

and both were falling upon the German trenches; how many was it? Less than two hundred yards away, optimistically. From what little he could see, peering through the lattice of the tunnel's gate, Felix didn't worry too much. It didn't seem the ground was all that wet. He knew, from those awful days last fall, just how much wet ground slowed things down, the muck of earth turned over and again, churned into a slurry with heavy, constant autumn rain grasped and sucked at boots plunged into it, amplifying the effort of a single step to that of Sisyphus. It was exactly like those dreams when he's running away from something, but all efforts produce no movement. So, dry ground was good. This stretch of ground furrowed with shell holes and shreds of tree stumps, led and rose, unevenly to a switchback of the German line, dug deep into the forward slope of the highest feature for miles around. If Fritz popped his head up out of those bunkers of his, well, he'd be able to see the entire show. Four divisions- the whole Goddamn Corps were waiting, up and down the line, many of them in saps like this one. Waiting for the second hand to finally tick, the walking barrage lifted, the symphony of whistles; waiting to step out into death.

This particular switchback faced more or less directly the camouflaged exit from the tunnel. It would be terrible if the enemy had sited machine guns there. A problem with that was every man in Six Platoon knew that the enemy had. Two machine guns, to be exact; water-cooled Maxims that turned thin air into a lead beehive. They knew, these men so precisely the layout of the trench in front of them because this morning it was their job to destroy it. The German lines on either side of the strongpoint which contained the machine guns described an almost ninety-degree angle. Moving towards it would be horribly like walking into the narrow end of a funnel. Each man waiting within who had gone "over the top" before certainly appreciated not only the protection the tunnel provided as they waited, but that it cut the distance to travel almost by half. That was why speed was key, as Lieutenant Thorncliffe had told them all, no use in squandering a head start so well gifted to them. Not only would moving quickly mean spending less time exposed in no-man's land, but taking those guns would reduce German firepower in the immediate area. With those guns gone, the rest of B Company's platoons could move to their objectives with little to stop them. Felix's rifle section would be first out. The snow, he thought, might even mean the ground was still frozen. God, it had been a cold winter, February in particular. Those short days were deceptively bright, seeming to make the crisp air sting all the more. Though that was nothing compared to those February nights. No, Felix corrected himself; not those, that. He couldn't recall ever being as bone cold as that night. There was a tap on his shoulder, turning him away from his post-box view of the war outside. He straightened immediately, a habit nearly two years in the making, seeing as it was the Platoon Commander.

"They're catching Hell out there, eh, Catscratch?" Thorncliffe had known these men- those few who remained- from first muster at Niagara Camp. If he dispensed with formality from time to time, it was done with a familiarity gained by enduring the same hardships. Not everyone in Six Platoon had a nickname, so it was a special recognition for Strachan.

"Yes, Sir," he nodded, his officer's casualness not being a two way street.

"Wouldn't it be grand if Arty's managed to do the job for us?"

"Stranger things have happened, Sir."

"Best not count on it, then," he said with a wry smile. "Just get your boys out and keep moving. Sutherland's rifle bombs should buy you some time."

Strachan nodded. "With any luck, Sir, we'll be in position before they get those guns up."

"Let's hope so." Thorncliffe had a moment of a far-away look. "Jesus, Catscratch, do you remember how it was there? Everyone being cut to ribbons outside Spoon Farm?"

Strachan remembered, alright. The Regiment's first action, what felt like a thousand years ago, in October. The preceding months of effort at great cost had pushed the Germans from front line positions they had held more or less since the war ground down to a stalemate. In 1914 grand, sweeping armies moving and manoeuvering across the landscape had met and smashed away at each other until both were too punch drunk to continue. Doctrine insisted on developing defensive positions until such time as enough men and materiel could be sent to the front for what was envisioned, even that early on, to be "the big push." This prophecy was touted as the only way to break enemy trench lines so that the open warfare more familiar to the powers that be could resume. It was nearly two years before all the pieces were in play to have a go at it. Which is what the fight at the Somme River begun way back in July had been all about. As a grand scheme, the battle failed, but persistent and near constant attacks had wrested some ground away from the invaders. Such that, by October, when the Regiment went up the line in earnest for the first time, the Germans were now fighting from positions which had been, at the beginning of it all, far to the rear. That fact had been used to reassure the men of the King's Own; they weren't to expect prepared defences. When the leading platoons of the attack came upon the road they had to cross and were able to see beyond, all there was was the farmstead and what barbed wire there was had mostly been mounted on frames, lattice-like and scattered across the frontage, more an impediment than a true barrier.

"Take and hold the redoubt known as 'Spoon Farm' and the crossroads in locality to support assaults on sections of 'Regina Trench'," had been the Regiment's orders that day, and now those in the van, Felix among them, were just beginning to believe they were going to do it, and without a lot of fuss, either.

Five and Six Platoons had walked straight into machine guns hidden behind the ruins of the high wall which enclosed the Farm. It was a dear price to pay. Felix remembered how, at first, the dust splattering around him seemed to be rain. That was, until Sergeant Merrick's back tore open, grotesquely ripped in half from hip to collar. Cutler had been right alongside Felix, with a stark look of disbelief which mirrored his own at what they had both just witnessed. He remembered it clearly, as if it played out, but slowly, in the theatre of his mind. It couldn't have been long after Merrick was cut down that Cutler was clipped in the shoulder, a slick warm spray that smelled of meat dappled Felix's tunic. Another step to his left and he found the ditch beyond the torn up road the platoon had been crossing when the firing started. Dragging himself on one arm, Cutler slid in behind him in a heap. The machine guns remained concentrated on the road itself. Five and Six Platoons, having moved through a stubbed field on the approach to the road without interference, took to the crossing with overconfidence. Flanked by ditches, the men were silhouetted on the horizon, under a midday sun. Now those who had made it across were trying to evaporate into the ditch, others staying put on the other side as in a matter of seconds the only thing left on the road were the wounded and the twisted heaps of the dead.

Felix had fought the temptation to turn around, look at the road and see who else had got hit, but instead kept his gaze forward. There was Spoon Farm, hidden behind that blasted wall, seven feet high. The only breach, a wide crack uneven and ragged, the rubble of the masonry a jumbled pile of chunks of disparate sizes pouring out around it was home to the machine guns, still chattering away. Through the gap it was just possible to see the farm's chateau, remarkably undamaged, its sheet smooth walls capped with clay tiles having borne the past two years better than much of the landscape. In itself it was hardly imposing, rather quaint and provincial. Peeking over the roof line the old trees of the farm's orchard showed themselves, some boughs broken by the abuses of war, the others shedding leaves in preparation of the winter that wasn't far off. In between was still more scrub field studded with barbwire traps. Cutler had gotten his shell dressing out and had it sopping up the mess of his left shoulder.

"I'll see if I can find a stretcher party," Felix had said.

"Don't bother. I'll be alright, but it hurts like blazes. I'd say you're more likely to need a stretcher if you go wandering about." He even managed a smile, though it was muted by pain. There was a moment, a slight stillness where the entire world seemed to exist of those machine guns tucked into the cracked wall and himself alone. It was sharply broken by a slightly vibrato bellow that scythed through the "whip" and "snap" of the German bullets.

"Six Platoon! Machine guns at the wall, rapid rate, fire!" It was Thorncliffe's voice, and there followed a few ragged shots, a few more, and then a steady bang in reply to the staccato fire from the farm. Felix got behind his rifle and felt some power return to him in pulling the trigger and working the bolt. The familiarity of the movement was comforting, somehow. Fifteen rounds a minute was rapid rate. He always counted the first five and topped up the magazine rather than firing out all ten at one go. It seemed that quite a few men had made it across, a succession of concrete puffs blossoming from the wall where the .303's had struck, and the fire was increasing yet. Felix had just fired a round and was cycling the action when someone crawled over top of him. Thorncliffe, pistol in hand, was making his way laterally along the ditch; towards where the road they had come across joined in a fork with the main road. Spoon Farm, slightly back from both roads was nestled in the crook they formed.

"Strachan," he said as he passed, "see who you can get from One Section and follow me. Fix bayonets."

Felix nodded, and went along the ditch himself, keeping low, finding his section mates and tapping them to follow the Sir. Park and Rankin he couldn't find. Lance Corporal Portland lay face down, his head-what was left of it- at the bottom of the ditch, his feet still touching the road. Almost insultingly, his left heel had been shot away as his body lay there, his kilt obscenely exposing his buttocks to the sky. Corporal Douglas was already with Thorncliffe, and Felix was soon alongside, having got Atherton, Taverly and Ferguson on the way. They crowded into the elbow of the ditch where it followed both roads.

"Right, is this it?" Thorncliffe had asked, "Alright then. Sergeant Olsen is in charge of Five Platoon. They and the balance of Six Platoon are going to keep fire on that bloody hole in the wall. We're following the road by way of the ditch towards the forward corner of Spoon Farm. It'll be a blind spot-look for gaps in the wire and call them out. Does everyone have bombs? Good. First one to the wall throws into the breach, everyone else who's made it, pour through once the first bomb goes; rush them at steel-point. Clear?" All nodded. Thorncliffe started crawling forward, his men right behind, keeping clear of the leaden duel between Sergeant Olsen's lot and the machine guns at Spoon Farm.

Strachan looked at Thorncliffe directly, the officer's face slightly drawn, shaded by the rim of his helmet and the half light of the tunnel.

"Spoon Farm was a while ago, Sir. I can't guarantee we'll know what to do; but we sure as Hell know what not to do."

Thorncliffe smiled out one side of his mouth.

"Pity the weather wasn't better. Fair cold, eh, Corporal?"

Strachan flinched, and looked at his sleeve where his chevrons stood out against the frayed and faded wool of his tunic, that's how new they were. He blushed a little. It was halfway pride in the title, halfway fear that in the next half-hour <u>his</u> decisions could wind up any of his eight men like Merrick, Portland or Cutler. If Felix had begun to understand anything about war is that there was little he could do to prevent these things. This lesson had begun in a shock of awakening at Spoon Farm and continued since. Culminating, perhaps, in that night; that February night. He shivered.

"Cold? Yes, Sir, but I've been colder."

Thorncliffe's sideways grin shifted into a full smile, and he winked. "That's the spirit, Catscratch."

Felix grinned in spite of himself. Cold? Yes, Sir, but not like it was. But that was it, Thorncliffe hadn't been there. Perhaps if he had been many things would be different, clearer. As it was, it was because Thorncliffe had been away in February that it had all happened, after a fashion.

Cold?

Yes, Sir, but not as cold as some. Some, left colder and starker than that damned February night.

Chapter II

France, February, 1917.

There was snow on the ground then, too. Weak but dazzling sunlight during the day ensured the snow remained in thin patches; the ground water in the shell holes and some of the poorer trenches thawing and re-freezing throughout the day. It guaranteed that no one's feet were ever completely dry and warm. Nothing strained the instincts of man the animal more than being wet. So ingrained in nature it was supposed that a desire to be shut of the constant discomfort of exposure is what inspired human beings to get down from the trees to start living in caves. Lieutenant Thorncliffe had taken pains, no doubt expressed to him through his superiors, to make regular foot inspections. The Regimental Surgeon, Captain Salinger's recent announcement was that the King's Own had the lowest number of cases of trench foot and frostbite in the whole brigade since they had come up to this area from the Somme. Prevention, it seemed to Felix, was worth a great deal. Although, just because one's feet weren't rotting away didn't mean that the damp cold wasn't pure misery. What was inestimably worse was being both wet and cold at a place and time where the prospect of dealing with either was far off. Like laying prone in a shell divot a little past midnight and twenty yards from the German wire.

In the trenches, the properly built ones, anyway, the wind could whip fierce overhead all it liked. What with everyone in the enclosed spaces and the ability to brew up tea over a small heater it could actually be cozy. At the very least was the notion of being able to move about, so that it didn't feel like his blood had congealed within the throughways of his veins into frosty crystals. He daren't move now, not even as the fiber of his body screamed out at him to do something to prevent what would surely be his shattering into tiny, icy pieces.

No. This close to the wire, no sound or movement was wise. Communicating with the rest of the covering party, Atherton and Robbins crewing the Lewis gun, was done by touch alone. Even then the three were as far apart as could be allowed. Huddling up to share warmth was one thing, but both Felix and Atherton knew the danger of bunching together too close. Help win the war, it was said, by causing the Bosch more bullets for each man dead. Robbins, newer to the front, hadn't had the same time to have picked up these things first hand, but he caught on quick enough in imitating what the old timers did.

Old timers. A stark matter of perspective that only a couple of months could impart as much experience as to be thought of as an old timer. Well, Felix mused, at that point you were either an old timer or you were dead. So, Robbins was alright so far, having not done anything monumentally stupid. He had come along just before Christmas with a replacement draft to shore up the losses the Regiment had taken since coming to France. Besides Spoon Farm, the days and weeks in between had borne witness to the slow, insidious and unpredictable phenomenon known as "trench wastage." Men, one or two at a time being caught by an errant shell, a sniper's bullet or any number of sickness or circumstance that shaved away at effective strength. Six Platoon, hovering at the fuller side of half-size had been given four new privates, which wasn't sufficient to fill out the missing files in a section, never mind a platoon.

It didn't help much that one of the four got himself killed almost straight away the first time up the line. Since then, and since there had been no indication of any further reinforcements, Felix and the rest of the veterans in Six Platoon had watched closely and tried to help the remaining three to stay alive. When the Regiment became active in the fall of 1915, it spent nearly a year both at home and in England for training. On arriving in France, it went through work-up training with short spells in the trenches closely supervised by experienced units before it could operate on its own. At first, losses had been made up from the Regiment's Holding Company in Kent. These men had been with the Regiment from day one, but who, for some reason or other had not made the cut when in preparation for the move to the front it solidified its organisation to four companies and had men left over. Although the Holding Company had missed the supervised orientation, their training had been as thorough as the men they were replacing, and in essence were brought up to speed through lessons imparted by those of the original draft. Like much else, the Holding Company was a limited resource which had been used up quickly. Such as that was, the infrequent and numerically inadequate appearances of reinforcements were largely men who just did not have the same length of training, which often proved problematic, if not fatal. It was clear to Felix that preserving strength now mattered a great deal for what he assumed with a near certainty was going to happen.

They were going to go up there; that bloody ridge in the middle distance. It grew lazily upward from its surroundings until it crested above the landscape; intimidatingly darker than the night sky framing it like a bas relief. The peaks in the folds of its rises and the silvery necklaces of wire shimmered in the bleary moonlight. Now was one of those times when clouds- even bearing snow- would be more ideal; anything to keep from being seen.

If Felix wasn't greatly concerned about Robbins, it was because Atherton had taken to him and made him his Number Two when he was assigned the Lewis gun. He had seen them, more than once, going through the loading, unloading and stoppage drills when the regiment was in the rear. By this point, they worked together as if part of the gun's natural mechanism. Pippin, on the other hand had struck Felix as a cause for concern. Not from anything he had done; but he was so slight and diminutive, with a broad, cheery face that he seemed younger than he claimed to be; almost childlike. A bit reserved, or perhaps intimidated by the bigger men of the platoon, he rarely spoke and when he did his voice was quiet and reedy. No small wonder he had quickly picked up the nickname "Squeak." Squeak's demeanour wasn't very soldierly, Felix decided; though not that he could afford too much criticism in that himself. The shyness and his stature made it seem that he wouldn't fare well in combat; that he was just playing at soldiers and would start for home the minute the game wasn't fun anymore.

Like it or not, Pippin was out here and nothing could be done. What's more, Felix could be wrong about him. After all, hadn't he volunteered for this patrol tonight as had the rest of them? Not like Coxwell, the other replacement. Felix had his measure too, a man who could achieve a great deal if he put the amount of effort as he did getting out of work into actually working. Patrols being voluntary, Coxwell was no doubt safe in the trenches, definitely warmer than the six men who had gone forward; probably asleep. The cold wore out the body, in either what it did to try to stay warm or the mind's efforts to cope. Sleep would be great, and that was dangerous; knowing that if he allowed himself he could sleep, here, despite the cold and certainly despite laying prone a little past midnight and twenty yards away from the German wire. It hadn't taken

Felix long to develop that peculiar talent of the soldier; that of being able to sleep anywhere, at any time, regardless of what was going on in his surroundings. Normally he needed dark and quiet to put his body to rest. These days, he could be in a hole half full of filthy water, while being rained on as the cacophony of war went on around him and be peacefully able to pass into his dreams.

Fatiguing as well were the demands of his senses. Though moonlit, the night sky was none too bright, blending silhouette and shadow so that the eye had trouble telling one from another. It didn't help that the imagination filled in the blanks, making each stump or slight rise into nefarious figures. Sound and smell were tested as well. Aside from the permanent miasma of decay, from time to time, Felix could smell tobacco smoke. One of those smells which people either find pleasant or disgusting, Felix had only recently become one of the former, having developed the habit for it. Almost as much as he longed for dryness and warmth or sleep-perhaps more- he wished to slake his desire for that satisfying, languorous feeling of calm which almost visually expressed with the release of an expanding cloud of blue-grey smoke. There was nothing to be done about that, either. Showing light would be tantamount to a suicidal action. All the while, whilst laying here with Atherton and Robbins he had strained to hear anything, particularly the other three returning. Where he was, there wasn't much he could be certain about any sound from the German lines. No doubt the scouting party, which had moved right up to the wire could make things out more clearly. Felix hated that, being on patrol that close to the enemy as to hear them talking. He had no German, so the times he'd experienced such things always felt like they were discussing him, unseen, mere feet away, and what they were going to do to him. It was terribly unsettling and he wouldn't like to admit it but it was havoc on his nerves. Every time he'd come back from these patrols, it took hours to settle himself. At least he could thank the cold for one thing. No one could tell if he was shivering with chill or shaking with uneasiness. While he still went out for these late night field trips, Felix was immensely glad to be here with the covering party rather than in Fritz's back pocket like the scouting party was.

Two days ago, another brigade had mounted a successful daylight raid on the Germans. Suitably impressed, the Division Commander had given carte blanche on subsequent raids. Lt Colonel Sinclair, the Regiment's C.O. then began putting his plans together for such a job. Raids differed from other types of offensive action in a very distinct way. The purpose was not to secure territory, but to cause a limited amount of damage. They became the epitome of keeping men at a high level of aggressiveness, and to keep the enemy off balance and over vigilant. Trench raids varied in size, from a small handful of men to so many troops involved that some raids could be counted as a miniature battle. One of the most successful raids, and one which would set the template for future operations and secure a peculiar reputation for Canadians, was conducted early in the war against German trenches near La Petite Douve Farm in November 1915 by the 7th Battalion, CEF. At the cost of one man killed and another wounded, the party of men of the 7th Battalion had struck a fierce blow against a defended line, taken a dozen prisoners and gained credible intelligence. It would make the reputation of that battalion, and of the Canadians as daring "raiders"; which also inspired other Canadian units to mount raids of their own in a spirit of one-upmanship. These subsequent raids improved on technique and helped to solidify the overall esteem of Canadian troops. The effect of such an operation could be enormous. It would first inspire confidence in the men taking part of their own abilities and their leadership. A successful raid showed them that the enemy could be taken by surprise and kept the ever crucial fighting spirit at a keen edge. Also, the enemy would be unbalanced, forcing them to improve their vigilance for such attacks, which wears on physical and psychological limits; especially if there was a prospect that armed men could drop into one's trench at any given time.

These six men now far into no-man's land were part of Colonel Sinclair's planning. The patrol's one task was to locate the sally ports built into the German wire. Finding them would mean not having to cut through the obstacle, and if their locations were certain the upcoming raid could use them to gain access to the sector of trenches they were to hit; provided they could move quickly enough to catch the Germans off guard. It was a foregone conclusion that these sally ports were over-watched by machine guns.

The possibility of being discovered grew with each inch closer to the enemy wire. One misplaced footstep; a surprise cough and the world would turn from dull and quiet to all light and racket as quickly as an electric switch. Tension of such moments wore on Felix. Oh, yes, so much better to be where he was even as his body warmth thawed the ground he laid upon, the frigid muck oozing through his uniform, further chilling him to the bone. About the scouts, Felix told himself reassuringly that they won't be too much longer. Ferguson was up there- and he knew what he was doing. Problem was he was doing it with Squeak, so very inexperienced and a new second lieutenant whose name Felix hadn't even learned. A transfer from parts unknown, he wore trousers instead of the Regiment's kilt; but new to the front nevertheless. With good fortune both this officer and Squeak would just let Ferguson do what he had to. That's what was probably taking so long. Felix didn't like it one bit but his instructions were to give the scouts twenty minutes and bring the covering party back alone if they hadn't returned.

They won't- they can't- be too much longer.

A single shot from the direction the scouts had gone shocked the silence. Felix turned to Atherton, in behind his Lewis, who shrugged. There followed a moment of stillness, as quiet as it had been before, but feeling more so, somehow. Then everything went inside-out, with a "whoosh" and "pop", flares made night instantly to day and up and down the line both sides began to fire. Several times Felix heard that sick making crunch of German grenades. They were being tossed, rather randomly, over the parapet in an effort to catch any interlopers.

He nudged Atherton, letting him know to get ready while begging that same fortune gone from just moments ago that the scouts would reach him before he had to pull out. Squeak was first back, daring to run through the flare light. Bullets tried to find him, kicking up the dirt at his feet and ricocheting off the thick strands of wire, making strange music.

"Put some fire on that point!" Felix ordered Atherton while Squeak dove into the divot. Immediately, short bursts from the Lewis gun answered the German fire, even if Atherton had nothing to shoot at. The first batch of flares faded, and now night blind, Felix didn't see Ferguson at first.

"Fall back!" he yelled at Felix, the terror in his voice undisguised "It's high noon on Main Street up there!"

Questions raced through Felix's mind-though there was not time for that just now. Only one mattered.

"Where's-"he started.

"Dead."

"Sure?"

"Yes. Let's get the Hell out of here, Catscratch!" It took him a moment, but the realisation hit him. As a Lance Corporal and given Mr. What's-his-name had been killed, Felix was now in charge of the patrol.

"Fern, Squeak, follow me. Atherton, fire the rest of that drum and meet us back at the secondary position. We'll all wait there and move back to friendly lines when it's safe." Before the next volley of flares went up, Felix rolled over and gained his feet, moving quickly though not in a straight line towards the rendezvous, not needing to check that Ferguson and Pippin were behind him, Atherton hammering away the last few rounds helping to obscure their movement. Repeated in short bounds between illuminations while the German guns searched for them, it took a long while to get there, but done in such a fashion it was the way the five of them got home.

Chapter III

The space heater in the nave of the old stone church was a homey comfort, even among the rubble of broken walls and a damaged roof grinning gap-toothed at the early morning sky. A gaslight was flickering atop Captain Lafferty's desk. Perhaps not a desk so much, having been unevenly cobbled together from old crates. The dancing light caught Strachan full on occasionally, revealing the steam rising from the damp wool. He was stood easy, the officer even giving him permission to smoke. Strachan wanted one, but couldn't trust his hands to light up, and he certainly didn't want to let on to Captain Lafferty how shaken he was. Not that it mattered, as the Captain was leaning over his blotter, pen in hand, piecing the events together as Strachan reported them.

Directly after crawling back into the trenches, dogged from the narrow escape and the hours it took to reach friendly lines, Felix had made his way down the line, past the support trenches to the little church which served at Regimental Headquarters.

More than anything, bone weary as he was, he wanted to curl up in a funk hole and finally sleep. His obligation, however, was to make a report to the adjutant and perhaps he might get to rest after the morning stand-to, three hours from now.

Captain Lafferty looked up from his writing, his face inscrutable. "This is a poor showing, Lance Corporal." Strachan nodded, he couldn't disagree. The patrol had been a complete wash. That much Lafferty had pulled together in the fact it was Strachan making the report, not Mr. Collier. He couldn't help notice the adjutant had to leaf through his daily reports to put a name to the dead officer. The Division was running a short school for platoon commanders and a selection of junior officers, which included Lt Thorncliffe of Six Platoon were tasked to attend. In the interim, the King's Own was sent a number of very new officers to get them acclimatised to the front before being permanently assigned. And now, one of them was dead. Captain Lafferty would later have to pull his file, note him as "struck-off strength; killed", send it on up to Brigade and that would be the last he'd think about it. He had done this, a regular part of his administrative position, too many times by now for it to have much of an effect on him. These papers representing dead men were to him just another type of filing. There was a certain bit of accountancy to it, which is how Lafferty approached his work. Before the war, he had been a bookkeeper for Sinclair's, the department store nearby the university he had graduated from. Now, Colonel Barclay Sinclair, his old boss, was his battalion commander. Detaching from identities and viewing his daily strength returns as a balance statement helped not let him dwell on what those losses entailed, in a sentimental frame of mind. He hadn't even asked Strachan for the particulars, which was fine with Strachan, as he wasn't certain of them himself.

* * * *

Right from the moment they came back over the bags, mouths dry and all else mud-drenched, and the night began to catch up. All the hours of remaining alert and physically tense for which the body only had so much reserve bled away and at once they all felt how cold it was, despite finally being in the trench, seated on the fire step. Felix was just reaching for his cigarette tin as Sergeant Douglas found him. It was right after Spoon Farm that Douglas had been quickly given a third stripe, to go along with the Military Medal he'd earned that day. That first machine gun he took on his own, bayonetting the gunner and bringing the loader down with a snapshot as he made to run.

"Well, Catscratch?"

Felix let the tin drop back into his pocket and waved, still out of breath. "Give me a minute, Sarge." He coughed, Douglas held out a bottle to him.

"Sorry it's nothing stronger than water. Might be rum in the morning if it sticks this cold."

"Thanks, Sarge. Water's fine." Felix drank and passed the bottle on. "We lost that officer."

"What do you mean, 'lost'? Did he bump into a tree and forget where he was?"

Nodding towards Ferguson, Felix said "Fern was up there when it happened, Sarge." Douglas raised an eyebrow to the other man.

"Didn't he trip up and have his rifle go off? Laying there, I was going to fetch him up, see if he was hurt, like, just when those flares ruined it for everyone. I sent Squeak back, and when I go back to the Sir, a burst chewed through him. 'He's had it' I says, and get on in behind Squeak, there, right?" Pippin only nodded.

Douglas blew air over his lips. "Poor bastard with us less than a day. What about the wire?"

"There were some good sallies up there, Sarge." Ferguson continued, "Well hidden, good use of the ground. Machine guns, obviously."

"Right-"Douglas started.

"But the officer had the notes with all the markings. There was no way for me to get it."

"Shit. Catscratch, get on to Regimental HQ and make your report. The rest of you, rack out for a bit. Stand-to at zero seven."

Grabbing his rifle, buttoning his pocket and replacing the knit cap he'd worn on patrol with a helmet Felix hopped down off the firing step and went along the duckboards to the rear. Half of them were under a thin sheen of ice where a puddle would be at daybreak, the others coated in frost which the hobnails in his boots failed to grip. Moving through a trench at times felt like an acrobatic stunt.

* * * *

Captain Lafferty was about to say something further, but was interrupted by Col Sinclair, who had just stepped past the shadows and appeared at the adjutant's desk.

"Not good news, indeed." Every man in the battalion knew Sinclair, at the very least by reputation if not association. His family's store catered in higher end furnishings, housewares and wardrobe. Many of those in the King's Own of lesser means may not have shopped there, but would know the attractive full page advertisements which ran in the Daily Star. Never to his face was he called "Bargain Barclay," though he was aware of the sobriquet. The irony suited his sense of humour. In actuality, the men very much admired him. His Presbyterian sense of fairness meant he could be as hard as nails or jovial and complimentary in equal measure. It was such that those on the receiving end knew themselves deserving of either admonishment or praise. Just as every man in the battalion knew him, he knew each man under his command. This was mostly thanks to Captain Lafferty's impeccable record keeping, as he used the adjutant's reports as crib sheets to jog memory on who was who under his command. Sinclair was revered because he wasn't just an adventuresome toff, he'd earned his spurs and a DSO with the Mounted Rifles in South Africa. It was right there on his clean, dry, freshly pressed tunic; a blue edged red ribbon accompanied by those representing the

King's and Queen's South Africa Medals. A captain then, his acts of courage were known, in keeping with his sensibilities, only to himself and those who wrote the citation. Released a brevet major, Sinclair began to become increasingly involved in the family business, taking it on completely in 1906 when the Old Man finally retired. The start of the war in Europe, that hot, heavy, long August three years ago had pulled hard at Sinclair. Without anyone to run the store, he was relegated to sit this one out. War is good for business, so it is said, but for men in Sinclair's line of offerings, shortages and war frugality scratched away at the bottom line. Staff increasingly became hard to hold on to and tough to replace, which he'd felt immediately after the government had called for volunteers at the start of it all. 1915 was going to be a bad year for Sinclair's Department Store. The war looked not only to continue, but become much worse the longer it went. Upon the announcement of the creation of a fourth division for overseas service, Sinclair had done enough waiting. "Bargain" Barclay reached his short arms into his deep pockets and funded his own battalion.

Activated in September of that year, the King's Own Canadian Scots drew volunteers from all over

Southern Ontario. Many were city boys who knew the store, quite a few- like Captain Lafferty- had worked for Sinclair's. As a matter of fact, Battalion Transport was largely made up of the store's own teamsters. Others had been provided from training depots and at Niagara Camp. They arrived in Kent the following May, full strength at just over eight hundred men, and in France with the 4th Division that August. Here it was now, February, and the Regiment was a lot leaner. Losses were close to three hundred officers and other ranks, most of those from the tail end of the Somme Campaign last autumn. Not nearly enough had returned to duty or arrived as reinforcements. Captain Lafferty's reports of all the comings and goings held the King's Own at a level edging on seventy percent effective.

This evening was fairly dire. Mr. Collier had been one of the very few subalterns sent to the Regiment, at a time when five of his sixteen platoons were without officers. The short course at Division for platoon commanders, although essential to the upcoming major operation in the spring, had pinched even further. Sinclair considered it a bit careless in afterthought. When the Second Lieutenant had asked to lead Six Platoon's scouting patrol, he'd demurred at first. Collier hadn't even gone out to his platoon, he'd been processing in with the adjutant, who must have told him about it. Sinclair knew Six Platoon as well experienced, one of his best; so if the young buck was eager to get some legitimate experience, he'd be well looked after. Collier himself had clinched it by telling Colonel Sinclair that he'd already been in France, with Brigade Headquarters, about ten miles back of the line since November. No wonder he had been keen to get out there, Sinclair granted, as he would have done the same. He may have had the makings of a good platoon commander, but such as it was, it was often those qualities that make a good officer are the ones most likely to lead to danger. Sinclair took a different view than Lafferty at all the faces and names who had come and gone. Not so much the adjutant's clerical perspective rather than the necessary, and firmly held belief that these deaths, each one individually, were for something. Perhaps not something tangible, but meaningful in that way nevertheless. Sinclair just wasn't sure he knew the answer to what that something was. It puzzled him every so often, as with Collier, when trying to put reason to it fell short.

"Let's see that map, Mr. Lafferty." The adjutant slid it closer to the lamp, and Sinclair poured over it, hand on chin pensively. "With nothing from Six

Platoon, that puts the rest of B Company in an awkward spot. Here's what we'll do. Reduce the raid to A Company only, but have Five Platoon of B Company provide support. There was no chance of recovering Mr. Collier, Lance Corporal?"

"None whatsoever, Sir. They were right up at the wire when it happened and we all came under heavy fire." Colonel Sinclair pursed his lips.

"Very well. Inform Mr. Picton that I'll see him at the Orders Group here at one hour after stand-down. Captain Lafferty, send a runner to 'A' Company headquarters with the same message for Major Daventry and his platoon commanders." The Colonel's eyes flitted over Strachan. "That will be all, Lance Corporal. Dismissed."

Strachan came sharply to attention, threw his best salute and turned on his heel. After collecting his rifle he stepped outside, a pale sky slowly washing out the stars. Five Platoon was entrenched to the left of Six Platoon's position, but to get there it required going along a communication trench further up the line if he wanted the most direct route, which, of course he did. The sooner he had delivered Colonel Sinclair's instructions to Lt Picton, the sooner it was Felix could finally be shut of orders to carry out, for the time being, anyway. That was the way of things in the army. It seemed that just as he believed his long day finally drawing close, he was handed just one more thing to do. While he wasn't best pleased about the failure of his patrol, the Colonel hadn't been harsh about it. A silver lining for Felix was that he wouldn't be part of the raid and could almost count on a night under cover in the trenches. Almost, he had added, because nothing in the army could ever be counted on. This had also come along with the lessons that this place with its ambivalent cruelty had handed to him- nothing was certain from one moment to the next and events swept up men and carried them along, helpless, powerless as in a strong tide towards the depths beyond the horizon.

At long last, he reached again for his tin. When he put his hand inside, though, all his smokes were sodden, useless. Felix allowed himself a whispered curse, and shrugging his rifle to his shoulder, tramped back up to the front.

Chapter IV

The Regiment was family. It was within the trappings of the badge they wore, the tartan of their kilts, the songs they marched to. It was how they identified themselves in this huge machine which for its purpose demanded homogeneity, but couldn't deny the human need for a distinct belonging. A soldier is led to believe that his regiment is best- an attitude which is actively encouraged. This may set a negative pretext for rivalries among regiments, but generally the effect is that in which if a man believes he is part of something highly valued he can be relied upon to perform as such. The bonds formed by men in their training while being indoctrinated into a well-established structure meant that support in disagreements in the barroom can be transmuted into devotion on the battlefield. Many of the pre-war regiments of the Active Militia which were to become part of the Canadian Expeditionary Force in the First Contingent lacked requisite numbers to form full battalions. As a result, and as part of a notion by Sam Hughes, Minister of Militia, to form an overtly

Canadian force, regimental identities were disallowed, and battalions were organised with no reflection of regimental heritage. A badge, in the form of a maple leaf embossed with the battalion number would become a rather generic identifier. While the result of this was largely positive- inspiring men to think and identify in a more national sense than regional, it also casually discarded the benefits which come with a strong link to tradition and heritage. This happened to the King's Own, which was a war-raised regiment and not based in any pre-existing unit of the Active Militia. Unceremoniously awarded the battalion number of 279, Colonel Sinclair had to fight to retain the aspects of identity he had created, to the point that the battalion number was used in official communiques alone; those within the Regiment referring to themselves and retaining the accoutrements of the King's Own Canadian Scots. For front line soldiers like Felix, the Regiment was the highest level of command they would have had a close intimacy with. Things such as brigades, divisions and corps would be much more abstract concepts. Sure, each man in the King's Own was meant to know to which of these higher formations the Regiment belonged and be able to name the general officers in command of them.

This knowledge went mostly unused due to the infrequent interactions between the rank and file and the higher-ups; particularly when they were at the front. It wasn't very common to have anyone higher than the Colonel to come see them, this far up the line. Not from, as it might have been supposed, for a lack of frequency of visits to the front from brass hats; more so that generals commanding such large formations as they did had so much more ground to cover, if they intended to do so in person. If communications were good, they would genuinely have less of a need, but a good general was one who would see his men in the field whenever the situation permitted. In the rear, at rest, though it was still infrequent, there was a greater possibility of spotting one. The Regiment was usually paraded, particularly during a long stay in billets, and always had some muck-a-muck to inspect them. Sometimes it was the Brigadier, at others one of his staff. Only very seldom was it the Division Commander and to see the Corps Commander was much like hen's teeth.

Even Colonel Sinclair couldn't be present with his men too much. He knew that there was a careful balance between sharing danger and interfering. Let the Company Commanders run their departments, Sinclair was "minding the store." His travels to the front line were done in a spirit of casualness, chatting and smoking, shaking hands and asking after family. Felix supposed it was very fatherly and it endeared the Colonel to the men all the more. Certainly it put to Felix's mind that his own recollection of such things was very dim and distant indeed. Entirely like the Colonel appearing in his fire bay-whatever they were doing at the time ceased as everyone gave Sinclair their attention, until it was waved away- was how he remembered the infrequent presence of his own father.

Felix may have been three or four; it was all rather vague, the last memory of them all together, when his world was a very small place. Consisting of the old cottage with the dirt track out front which led down to the village and a rough, rocky garden in the back, the universe according to Felix then was bordered by crags and bens, burns and braes, sealed in underneath a perpetually heavy grey sky. For a young boy, his father's absence and short visits were confusing. Where was it he could possibly go in between? Each time Da left, and each time he returned he came by way of the village. Ma would send him and Morrigan out to the stone fence by the roadway on certain days, he and his sister watching the figure of their father coming up the slight rise, always sharply turned out, the brass buttons of his tunic and toes of his boots gleaming, his gait a swagger that set the tassels of his sporran moving back and forth with the rhythm of his pace. A child's sense of such things being all that he could bring memory from, Felix was aware that there as something immensely good about these times. Ma would be more cheerful, and less likely to scold. It was all she could do, she would say about it, left on her own with two rascals and the bairn needing her every minute God sends, so could you be a bit more helpful, please? When Da was home, that changed, and besides that, there was something more. He hadn't really known until long after the fact what it was that made one particular image clear. Felix and his sister shared the straw mattress on the floor in the second room. A tiny peat stove warmed it a little, but the floor was always like ice in the night. Their parents' bed, not much less meaner than theirs was at least off the surface, suspended on a rope frame, but at the moment it was empty, the room still and dark. A flicker of light around and through the slight cracks in the door and its frame and hushed voices beyond it were reassuring that everything was as it should be, despite not being able to distinguish what was being said. Ma's voice, soft and light, was interrupted by baby James gurgling away in her arms. Da's was deeper, a fine baritone that no whisper could really hide, inflected by the hissy whistle of the way his "esses" tumbled out. What it was that Felix had felt then, and had only recently discovered was that he had known, that young, what it was to feel safe. As safe as to be assured from all harm; but only so long as the moments creating that feeling lasted. This was what stood out more for him, that it was gone so soon. Felix's last memories of Banchory were beyond the ones of comfort and safety. Only old enough to grasp context, he had only the impression that something was very wrong; he had never seen Ma greet so much as she did before they left the old house for the last time. Not until, that was, he had left the new one for Niagara Camp.

The company, as with Felix in 'B' Company was much like that, a camaraderie of workmates. Captain McCormack was the boss, generally aloof and often surrounded by his small staff of signallers and orderlies. The Captain managed 'B' Company in such an off-hand way mostly because he strove to work the information Captain Lafferty and the orders Colonel Sinclair gave him into the best possible resolution based on his own understanding of what was in front of his positions. Very much a big-picture man, Captain McCormack entrusted 'B' Company's day to day running to Lieutenant Aldridge, his second-in-command and the Company Sergeant-Major, Gordon. As 2 I/C, Aldridge was often away sorting work parties for trench maintenance or supervising distribution of ammunition, rations and the mail-the outgoing he censored- among countless other tasks and minutiae a rifle company required to function, and for which the Captain just didn't have the time to devote to himself. Thankfully, omnipresent among all four platoons was CSM Gordon. If 'B' Company were a workplace, Sergeant-Major Gordon was the shop steward. Whenever someone was about to do something daft, Gordon always seemed to be there, as if clairvoyant. The platoon officers, though senior to him by nature of their commissions, listened to his advice and generally concurred with his opinions. Gordon was an ex-twenty year soldier, he had been to India as well as South Africa. It was Gordon who had Christened 'B' Company "Buckshee Company." The word meant "something left over, spare, obtained for free" and was taken from the melodious Hindu terms that men who had been and gone used to pepper their shop-talk with. As it always seemed that it is one's own Company always getting the short shrift, the name suited that subtle nature of self-deprecation unique to soldiery. Gordon knew intricately how the system worked for having worked within it so long. No goldbrick scheme could get past him. He knew all the tricks, had tried a few in his time and was suspected of having invented some of his own. A good Sergeant-Major like Gordon was a blessing to the running of a company. Captain McCormack could throw himself into strategy and Lieutenant Aldridge could run the administration as long as a man like Gordon was seeing to how well the individual pieces were working.

Home, for Felix, however, was really the platoon. These were the men with which everything was experienced in common. Rare was the day that they didn't all eat together, sleep in the same holes, endure the weather- fair or worse. When in action, they fought closely together, so reliant on one another; the war at that distance reducing itself to lowest common denominator; they fought for each other. A loss within the platoon was felt strongest by those who remained, those of other platoons or companies within the Regiment seeming more like the news of the death of a distant relation. Spoon Farm had, in an astoundingly short time broken down what had taken a year to build. When the Regiment was pulled out of the line two days after that fight, the whole of 'B' Company had been reduced to sixty-four percent of its full strength, including losing half its officers. Six Platoon had lost nine dead and fourteen wounded from which had been a full strength of thirty-six. Besides Sergeant Merrick, Corporals Darlington and Shaw had been killed, as well as three lance corporals. The platoon had nearly been decapitated, and for the time being it had organised itself into two large sections instead of the usual four.

Now there were vacant spaces left by those who had "gone West." Putting the effectiveness of a short-handed platoon aside, the very fibre of it had been changed. There would be no more sharing of the wonderful, but slightly stale cakes Chase's mum would send him, or having to endure Sergeant Merrick's awful jokes. Not only was it that the trickle of reinforcements Six Platoon received were inadequate in number, the immediate prejudice of the remaining original members was that the new men couldn't repair these losses specifically because they weren't the personalities of those they were replacing. They were strangers in a time and place where familiarity could equate survivability. Some in

Six Platoon might have rather gone on at a reduced strength rather than deal with an unknown quality. Ideas such as these were academic, anyway, the army not making a habit of consulting opinion.

Lieutenant Thorncliffe had done his level best to keep the platoon functioning despite the losses it suffered. The contraction in number of sections had made it easier to fill vacancies among NCO's. Corporal Norton was the only surviving original section commander, Tapscott, the platoon's senior Lance Corporal took over for Douglas when the latter was promoted and became the platoon sergeant. With these limited operations of late- patrols and raids- often ad hoc units would be cobbled together on requirements and available manpower, so keeping a tight organisation at all other times helped with an essence of consistency. In this way, Thorncliffe was conscientious to only invoke changes which were absolutely necessary to the continued functionality of his platoon. His men loved him for that, just another way in which the Lieutenant had always been there for them, as he had been at Spoon Farm. Each man remembered, very distinctly and in their own way Thorncliffe's orders when they had come under fire for the first time. "Six Platoon! Machine guns at the wall, rapid rate, fire!"

A certainty, real or forced-and Thorncliffe himself didn't know for sure- in his voice had shaken Six Platoon from the Hellish phantasm they had just walked into. It had felt as luck or instinct which helped him in having the right idea of what to do next, the clarity to implement it and the wherewithal to personally lead his men to the objective. This foundation of capability and fortune had been augmented by a strict list of qualities Thorncliffe had been obligated to adopt. Left last on that list for emphasis rather than lack of precedence was one quality, a concept which could only be mimicked until the time came to apply it in earnest. It demanded an effective platoon commander be "Bloodthirsty"; that he be forever conniving ways to kill the enemy and inspire a like spirit in his men. Thorncliffe had been carried so far on applying himself to all principles of his position on intellect. Words of command he'd been trained to use were intentionally abrupt and aggressive, their delivery meant to be an amplification of the same, and that had helped a fair deal. That his men had been conditioned to respond to such orders equally abruptly and aggressively carried a larger remaining balance on being able to get the job done. Rushing the machine guns and then flushing out the charming little farm house leaving the handful of Germans dead where they lay was the only thing which could, and did, create the psychic shift from merely understanding a dread concept to believing it unconditionally. Restraints usual to society had been lifted, but the individual had to be given such a demonstration as Thorncliffe had for them to become purposefully single-minded and violent. A focus on the present gave little room for the alarming thought that no one had told him where the mental switch was which would reverse such deep conditioning when it was time to get back to ploughing.

When Felix thought of home these days, rather than the distant image of his uncle's vineyard in Niagara, a place he hadn't seen in a year and a half, or even the long-ago and imperfect vision of the farm cottage in Banchory, his thoughts were towards Six Platoon. It was to this further surrogate home that he arrived, after delivering the Colonel's message to Lieutenant Picton, silently wondering which of the men of Five Platoon he'd seen on his way would still be alive tomorrow. With only a few minutes before the day would begin- with the morning stand-to- Felix reported to Sergeant Douglas.

"What took?" Douglas asked.

"Bargain Barclay had me run an errand to Five. They're going out tonight supporting 'A' Company's raid. The rest of us are out of it."

"Well, there's a bit of good news." He checked his watch, "Best get along back to One Section; it's almost time for the 'hate'."

The 'hate' is what the men called the twice daily effort to remind everyone that this was a war, though there was plenty else, in sight sound and smell which provided evidence of that. Tactically, they were prudent. As the most likely times to attack were at sunrise and sunset, having the firing trenches fully manned and with weapons ready ensured preparedness to defend against any such attack. Ironically, this was the practice of both sides, meaning that when the front was quiet, as it could be a great deal of the time, as it was now relative to all else, two times a day across the meandering distance of no-man's land, two great armies engaged in a staring contest. That, and it meant that any other time, usually about twenty hours' worth of any given day was running a tie for being the next most likely time for the enemy to attack. Sometimes quiet was prelude to the storm, and that such a shift could occur in an instant, it led to a constant thread of tension along the front line.

The routine of the daily stand-to helped in a way to provide normalcy where that was a rare commodity.

Felix nodded to Corporal Norton as he came into his Section's fire bay, and seeing that he had one lit, cadged a cigarette from him. Lighting up, he had that queer sensation that the smoke was all his body needed; why he had felt so tired and dragged out because of its absence. A rare pleasure it was to allow this relief, was Felix's immediate thought, followed by the guilt he had knowing his mother would wallop him for smoking. What an odd thing to think about, he shrugged to himself, getting ready to mount the fire step. He laughed silently at the image of his mother, oatmeal spoon in hand whilst standing on the deck of an ocean steamer, waiting to dock at Le Havre so she could find her way to the front and cloup him. In some ways, he feared his mother and her spitfire temper more than the prospect of German steel ever could.

Sergeant Douglas checked his watch one last time and gave Private Nelson the signal to begin. Nelson tucked the bladder under his arm, inflated it with one great breath, and then squeezed the collected air over the chanter's reeds. As began every morning when the Regiment was in the line, its pipers, dispersed among the platoons, filled the blushing sky of dawn with the whine and hum of martial airs. One part an act of defiance, the other was letting the enemy know who they were, hopeful that they were aware of the Regiment's reputation and were intimidated by the sounds of "Cock o' the North"- as if to say "It's the King's Own you're dealing with, Fritz. Best mind your manners."

Nelson's playing was accompanied by a bash and rattle, the men's kit shifting about as they took their posts at the parapet; and the un-synchronistic hiss-snap of bayonets being drawn and fixed over muzzles up and down the line. The tune came to an end, and there was nothing but its fading echo on the slowly brightening sky. No-man's land returned to its uneven form from the receding shadows of dawn. Ugliness in rough ground strewn with litter, steel and wood and flesh grew in composition until it was in full focus. Nothing moved, except whatever the rats disturbed. They stood like this, still and silent, watching for any sign of trouble, until the sun had gained purchase in the morning sky. Sergeant Douglas, moving along the fire bays spotted CSM Gordon waving at him to stand down his men. As if automatons, the men, once relieved, slid back down to the firing step, the odd numbers among them pulling their rifles apart for cleaning, the evens waiting until they were done, a drill that kept weapons in good condition while not sparing too many at a time. Felix used the weighted chord to pull through the barrel, scratched away a small fleck of rust on the foresight and then he wiped the steel down with the chamois he kept in his pooch, the large pocket in the front of the cotton khaki cover worn over his kilt. Once he'd snapped it back together, locking the bolt back in place and fitting the magazine, Felix ran through the function test and was satisfied. A few yards along and scraped out of the earth beneath the fire step was just the place he wanted to be. He dragged himself towards and nestled up inside his funk-hole, with his helmet and boots still on. In spite of his body and clothes being still cool and damp, he finally stopped shivering; the deep sleep of exhaustion whisking him off immediately.

Chapter V

Before him was something at once as familiar as it was strange. A shallow valley played out into the distance, reaching the cotton flecked azure sky in gentle rolls, only interrupted by a hillock overgrown with trees just that much darker than the grass around it. This, stretching out beyond the range one pair of eyes could see, no one had tended, so it looked after itself. The long stalks were tufted with crowns of seed waiting to take flight on the honey-sweet breeze to begin anew. Such a current carved rifts in the singular green, played them this way and that, surprising with flashes of red where the randomness of Creation had stood the flowers, it seemed, wherever it pleased them. With such a deep and rich hue, velvet and radiant, why wouldn't they be pleased with themselves? They had accomplished, in just being themselves more beauty than many things could only hope for in a lifetime. It was a bit of a shock, then, when the boot came down and crushed one of these flowers at the stalk. So shocking, disturbing the vista, that he didn't realise at first that the boot belonged to him; almost unrecognisable as such, the worn leather was wrapped in strips of hessian cloth cut from old sandbags. The shape was perverted into irregularity with clots of mud, soaked black by a viscous sludge of water and filth- all the filth of the world. Now, pinning the trampled beauty of the flower underfoot, the muck flowed outward from where he stood, the grass withering silently where it touched that in moments the scene was gone, replaced by a lifelessness in the lustreless parched shade of old rusty-brown photographs.

His attention wavered from the field to a distant, yet definite sensation of a boot pressing against the small of his back. Lightly but deliberately nudging, the soft kicks made Felix aware that the valley was receding like he was being removed from a picture which he had never actually seen. As he turned over, he found Corporal Norton leaning over him, blocking the light.

"C'mon, Catscratch, time to get up and earn your pay."

"A buck fifteen? Keep it, Nort. In fact, I will pay you five dollars to let me sleep another twenty minutes."

"Tempting, but it's really not up to me. Sarn't Major says you've gotta see the Captain."

"The Captain? What for?" He sat up now, still a bit bleary, took his helmet off with one hand, scratching the matted crop of his hair with the other.

"Didn't tell me. Mind, not that anyone ever does. Maybe something about that dead officer."

"Collier?"

'That was his name?"

Felix nodded "Guess you heard already."

"Awful, ain't it, doing something that mindless first time out? At least he did us a favour in not getting the rest of you killed while he was at it. Got himself out of the way before he'd have a chance to get anybody killed, you ask me."

"I wouldn't know. Got a smoke?"

"Yeah, your last one- I got no more to spare until we get the rations up. And what do you mean, you don't know? You were there, weren't you?"

"There, but not nearby. I didn't see it, but I sure did hear that shot. Well, everybody did, and it was time to skedaddle." Lighting up, Felix tipped his helmet as he stood to gather himself. "Thanks awfully, Squire."

"Smartass." Was all Norton could manage in response before Felix made tracks, again, but this time for Company Headquarters.

Right after stand-down that morning, Captain McCormack was returning from his post outside, to his dugout- and coffee- to find his telephone rattling away in an incessant clicking drone, the caller urgently cranking the signal switch without pause. He lifted the receiver after nearly tumbling down the steps and once again narrowly missed tripping up on the shallow ditch at their base- a handy thing for defence against grenades, but a bane to the ankles of a rushing man.

"Buckshee. Go ahead."

"Scott?" Captain Lafferty's voice came through.

"Yes, Doug?"

"We have a bit of a problem." McCormack couldn't be sure whether it was a weak connection or if his old chum was whispering.

"You're going to have to send another patrol out. Tonight. Time it with 'A' Company's raid."

"What's the objective?"

"Collier's body." Lafferty hissed.

"Doug, don't be daft. I'm not sending another lot out that close to the wire to the same place two nights in a row."

"Let me explain. I don't like it any more than you do, but it's critical you send a party to locate Mr. Collier's remains."

"Why is he so Goddamned important?" McCormack catching himself in the act of being angry at a dead man.

"He had," Lafferty dropped his voice and spoke more slowly; his pace with the words allowing them to hang for individual consideration on the gravity of their meaning, "copies of the Brigade's maps with him."

"Christ."

"It is how he got the Old Man to let him go on last night's show. Brigade, Division and Corps are really going all out on maps. Something about getting copies of operations maps to smaller organisations-platoons and sections. So, Sinclair sends him out to get the notes he needs- but nobody told Collier that he was supposed to leave the marked maps behind and add to them when he returned." Lafferty's head almost ached at being faced with such crushing irony. Complete maps didn't leave the trenches exactly for this reason. "Fritz finds them, he's got every trench, sap, headquarters, and gun pit for the entire Brigade's frontage."

"And where we know their stuff is as well."

"Get good men on this, Scott. 'A' Company's raid will be a perfect distraction, but above everything, all efforts must be made to get those maps back. This operation in the works is huge- we can't allow them to get their eyes on what we're up to."

McCormack sighed, resigned. "I understand, Doug. I'll call you to let you know the result."

"Good luck." Lafferty wished as he rang off.

'B' Company's commander wondered to himself if it was too early in the day to have started swearing, and decided it probably was. That being the case, it was probably too early in the day for a nip; so he called for the Sergeant Major instead.

Thus it was, shortly after that Strachan was again presenting himself in front of an officer.

"I want you to understand," McCormack had begun, "the critical importance of what I'm going to ask of you." The Captain looked at Strachan eyes on, a devoutly serious appeal of one man to another, beyond the station one had over the other. "In good conscience, I won't order you to do it-all the same it must be done." He took a heavy breath and laid out to Strachan the grave nature of Lieutenant Collier's oversight and that something be done to correct it. The light, fairly muted in the Company dugout to begin with grew darker around the edges of Strachan's vision, in league with a sudden shock of cold, his stomach wanting to fold over on itself. Captain McCormack went straight on with the business at hand, unaware from outward appearance that the man he was addressing desperately, sincerely, wished to escape his own body.

"I need a four man patrol. Take volunteers who have the most time in patrolling. Nothing is to be sacrificed for opportunity to gain experience. Ideally, Lance Corporal, at least one man in this party will have been on last night's patrol to act as a guide. This is highly unusual, and incredibly dangerous, but I wouldn't be asking if it wasn't also entirely necessary. I want this done quickly and at minimal risk. Travel light, pistols and rifles only- and only to be used as an absolute last resort. One more thing- each man will draw one Mills bomb from Company stores before going over." The taking of grenades on patrol, to the best of Strachan's recollection had not ever been given such emphasis. He spoke up.

"Sir?" to which McCormack lifted his hand.

"If this patrol can't, for any reason, reach or recover those maps; if they cannot be reasonably returned to our lines, then they must be destroyed." Strachan's stomach dropped again. The Captain's gist was clear enough: Tear up the maps even if it meant tearing up Collier's remains.

"I will expect these four volunteers here in one hour's time for a briefing and forced rest. Lance Corporal Strachan, even if you decide to opt out, I would appreciate your presence at the patrol briefing for your insight on the ground to cover." Captain McCormack then flicked his eyes to the dugout door- in effect an army horse blanket hung to block light- a hurried and instructive look. Strachan made himself scarce.

At once alone, McCormack took a moment. Circumstances had put him, well below his thirtieth year, in a very delicate office. He opened the trunk kept beside his desk and pulled from it his notebook. Bought in Paris of a fine shop, its pages were crisp, eager to have the nib of the fountain pen (a gift, last Christmas to all officers from the Colonel) scratch deep, richly black lines upon its virgin surface. McCormack was especially fond of this pen; the act of drawing, to him, just as satisfactory as the results produced. Thinking ahead, he wanted to see if he could find enough good pieces of salvage to make a slanted surface, or as best he could get to a drafting table. The young Captain had a first in drafting- and had been just about to begin higher studies in engineering when the war began. McCormack had paraded with his school's cadets, with the accountant Doug. A foregone conclusion that they join, among all the mates, names and vague recollections now long ago moved to other units, or a permanent address; he was taking classes to what he hoped would be a commission in the Engineers when events took him elsewhere. A bill had gone up, flashily calling out to a new regiment. Doug would be going, he concluded, Bargain Barclay being behind the whole thing, and he could name half a dozen more who'd be pulled. The prospect was an immediate commission, and to "be overseas at first priority." Scott wasn't thrilled with the notion of the infantry. His decision to join the King's Own may have had roots in keeping up with his chums, but it was his ability to rationalise that it was infantry which the war needed most which made it a practical decision rather than an emotional one. Justifying it as such was one thing, having it go beyond a position on the Colonel's staff was another.

Three days after signing his papers for overseas service, he had been called to see Colonel Barclay. A sitting room at a riverside inn, just beyond the guard house of Niagara Camp had been made into a Regimental headquarters; and not unintentionally, keeping the only place in any distance that sold beer out of reach of the rank and file. McCormack had been brought in, the Colonel holding audience from a plush, high backed leather chair behind a baize - topped, leather edged desk, for all the world, with the lit log fireplace behind him, like a prop in a floor display of his own store. Perhaps the flags at either side of the mantle and the handful of uniforms standing about were exempt from sale. Besides the Colonel, there was Major DeVere, his deputy, the Regimental Sergeant Major, along with a couple of chaps McCormack hadn't met. Lafferty, now in his new uniform of khaki tunic- the pips of his new rank standing in a row of three on each epaulette, a polished Sam Browne belt- still with an empty holster- and the richly deep green of the chosen Regimental tartan-Hunting Sinclair- of a kilt so fresh from the tailor it still sported the creases of the hot press, had caught McCormack a side glance, and risked a cheery wink.

"Mister McCormack," Sinclair had said, running through the tiny collection of papers which already occupied his file.

"Yes, Sir."

Still reading, the Colonel had then said, "Haven't much need of a draughtsman. I will tell you what I do need, young man. I need gentlemen of character and courage to inspire these men to their duty as soldiers. I need smart men who can make the right decisions regardless of circumstance. Do I have one of these men standing before me, Lieutenant?"

"I'd like to find out myself, Sir."

"Excellent. My Number Two Company needs a good commanding officer. Go set up your headquarters and establish your staff. Report to the adjutant after roll call tomorrow. Dismissed, Captain McCormack."

About maps, that they were missing, if that were the only issue, wouldn't have been a problem. McCormack could draw the Brigade's frontage from memory. Wrapping it up in an envelope and dropping it on Jerry's doormat; therein lay the rub, and the impetus to the final decision, before anyone else came down the stairs, to reach into the trunk again and pull the bottle of amber liquid free, pouring a good lot into his tin coffee cup. Only after he felt it burn down to his insides did he uncap the ink and set to drawing whatever he found in his imagination.

Felix's head swam. Partly from fatigue- a sensation of fogginess that grew every moment spent on the line, dribbling away from a finite reserve. Without even knowing how long he had slept that morning before Corporal Norton had woken him, there had been, certainly, less than two hours of that precious luxury in the past twenty-four. The other part, of course, lay within what Captain McCormack had asked of him. While the Captain may have left his participation optional, Felix could not see how he might request others to go and stay behind himself. There was no question, as far as he was concerned; the job was his to do. Perhaps McCormack's offer had been not much more than a formality, as things such as this usually were. While the both of them knew Felix couldn't refuse, it was still appreciated that the officer had kept the pretense of choice. Felix knew that it hadn't been done so that Captain McCormack could avoid the responsibility of giving a direct order. Time he had spent under his command had provided first hand evidence of the contrary.

The appearance of optional participation was the closest McCormack could get to being apologetic without overstepping the bounds of military courtesy. Sure, if Felix had refused, as all his instinct had begged of him, Captain McCormack would have lived up to his word and excused him. The issue was whether his sense of self-preservation would be enough comfort to be able to live amongst men sent out into peril in his place; particularly if any of them failed to return. It wasn't, and that was all there was to it, he was going out again. With that matter out of his hands, Felix's next trick would be to find three others just as circumspect as he to go along with him on what had to be the fool's errand to beat all.

Chapter VI

If trenches were just that- ditches running lengthwise across contested ground, it'd be a fair deal easier to remember whereabouts. Practicality and tactical necessities had seen these defenses grow in scale, evolve, incorporate a defense in depth of successive trench lines connected by perpendicular communications trenches. Now it was that several subterranean walkways moved in one direction or the next, intersected at points with an opportunity to go in another way altogether. In consideration of minimising casualties, none of these trenches or paths described a straight line. The most extreme example of this was the forward most line-the "firing" trenches- which were built in a pattern of bays and traverses at right angles; a landscape feature in a Grecian key. Lines further back and the communications trenches tacked and gybed less rigidly, but every way meandered at least a little bit. It wasn't from soldierly humour that street signs existed here, they were a genuine need. Some trenches were directional- keeping one way traffic also reduced confusion, so when it came all together as a system it was as complex as downtown blocks. Simple but familiar-or at least memorable- names had been given to all of these inter-webbed lines and really with that, the idea of living underground reached a certain level of adaptation. Which meant that when Sergeant Douglas was preparing to meet Six Platoon's section commanders he was at platoon headquarters, a rearward bay in the firing line at the junction of Upper Victoria Park Avenue and Front Street. After stand-down, with weapons cleaned and sentries posted, the day in the life at the front settled into routine. One such was the trickle-down effect of the days' plans and occurrences finally reached the platoon level, requiring platoon leaders to get pertinent information to their men. Sergeant Douglas had set up his special "tommy cooker" on a ledge which occupied a third of the platoon bay's front facing wall. A tommy cooker was normally a tiny field stove, burning paraffin or Sterno or a foul smelling solid tablet for individual use. Douglas had contrived to improve his. It used three cans of fuel instead of one and had a custom built grill- a piece cut from the corrugated iron of the type used to keep the trench walls and dugouts from collapse, and had been hammered flat and punctured by the smith in

Battalion Transport. The effect was a hotplate upon which more than one cup at a time could be put to boil. The rule was, Six Platoon NCO's who would come by for the morning chat could use the grill, but were responsible for bringing their own brewing kit.

Six Platoon's headquarters was as much as it could be an office this far up the line. There was no dugout here, in a grand sense, but opposite the ledge at which Douglas was lighting the fuel was a shallow scrape. Perhaps three feet deep and slightly lower than the trench floor and shored up with sandbags and iron sheets, the alcove was an optical illusion of a shaft entrance missing the shaft. More than permitting a workspace, it gave a place to keep telephones and paperwork from the elements. Folded to one side of the alcove was the sling back beach chair Thorncliffe's batman, Lance Corporal Sweeny had managed to bring into every billet the Lieutenant had been to since the start of it all. Orders were given and morning tea taken in the lounging comfort of the chair. Such a thing gave a reassuring casualness to the moment to moment uncertainty of this type of war. Lieutenant Thorncliffe could be counted on to spend his nights here, sleeping quite easily; but to hand where he should be a great deal closer than the platoon HQ dugout slightly arrear; if the night weren't to pass quiet. Douglas noted to himself to be sure to bring it off the line, the Sir due to rejoin them when they returned to billets.

Where Douglas was standing, although currently pressed into service as a tea-room, was where Six Platoon was properly commanded. The ledge provided enough space for Lieutenant Thorncliffe to write out orders and requests- either the daily back and forth, but on the fly as need be. The rest of the wall, besides the ledge held a recess in which the platoon reserve of small arms ammunition- hundred counts of the dependable .303 calibre rifle cartridge- was neatly stacked in wood boxes. In between ledge and recess, a proper fire-step led up to the periscope mount, a handy box wedged into the sandbagged parapet, its angled outline broken by disused bags, one of them a shroud on the trenchward side. This would allow a trench periscope to be placed without being obviously revealing. This concealment, however, restricted the ability to pan the scope, so a full 180 degree panorama wasn't quite possible.

Once again, the sun's brightness belied the bone cracking cold, and since the détente of midmorning, puffs of frosty breath and steam of hot drinks were the only things cresting the apex of the trenchline.

Norton and Tapscott were waiting on their tea with Douglas, who had just told them that Captain Salinger, the Regimental Surgeon, had not approved a rum ration this morning. Both section commanders grumbled, but their sergeant raised a good point.

"They'll rotate us out soon, probably tomorrow. 'A' Company puts in their raid tonight, back behind the lines by dinnertime Thursday."

"Can't say I envy them," Norton said, still not satisfied with the temperature of his tea, having tested it with grubby fingers poking out of a cropped wool glove, "Full moon tonight. It'll be like climbing onto the stage from the orchestra pit."

"Well," Tapscott ventured, "if it is a full moon, only the lunatics would have asked to go."

"Fair enough." Not that Douglas minded the joke, but there were more points to go over. "Tap, you're duty section. Have men ready to go with Lieutenant Aldridge for carrying parties. Sarn't Major says light stuff, rations more likely. Nort, be prepared to shift your men left while Two Section is short. There's not been a lot going on across the way. Reports are mainly of them digging and improving their positions. The engineers may be coming through our platoon lines this morning." There was nothing new to this, Sappers were a daily feature on the line. Much like civic workers, they showed up, inconvenienced right of way and accomplished a great deal of work of which the cynic only observed men leaning on their tools. They had been setting up for something, but were very contrite on the matter. An attitude more perhaps for the Sappers' wish to impress with the finished article rather than being obstinate or secretive. This tour up the line, though, they had been coming up through Eight Platoon, directly on their right.

Sergeant Major Gordon, who had briefed Douglas had done it in a hurry as he was dealing with the situation which had caused a change in the engineers' commute. Part of last night's fusillade had been a handful of trench mortar bombs which had struck mostly behind the trenches; though one had hit and collapsed part of the communication trench leading up to Eight Platoon's patch. Two men were missing, and the digging out would take some time. By chance, Douglas passed on to his men, the mortar had landed in a very delicate place.

"Damn it!" Corporal Tapscott spat. "That's what, four times this year?"

Douglas nodded, his attention on the cooker. "Four sounds about right."

"Out of what- a couple of shoots a week- the same rate as ours."

"Okay."

"The odds are against it not being deliberate."

"Where did you learn to add?" Douglas started, but Tapscott went right over him.

"They're making it so we can't even shit in peace!" Which was the first thing Felix heard as he turned off Upper Vic Park, back in his platoon and now in the midst of the NCO's meeting.

"What's that?" He asked. Douglas held sway and answered.

"Eight Platoon's latrine was hit." Felix avoided a quip, not really feeling up to a crude joke; as much as there had already been at his expense this morning. It was noticed.

"You don't look so good, Felix." Sergeant Douglas said with genuine concern. The young man was pale, besides the mud, dragged down by more than the weight of his webbing. Felix dutifully relayed to the three his understanding of current events and plans for the immediate future.

"You're going to have to get them from Six. Eight lost two and are still digging out Upper Yorkdale; Five's on the raid."

"Wouldn't have thought to ask another platoon." Felix said, sincerely.

"Does that loyalty go section deep?" Tapscott asked "Because my boys are 'it' today."

Felix nodded. "Don't think it'll be a problem. New guys are out-so- Fern, that's a cinch, Brentwood, O'Leary. I'd prefer not to take Atherton from the Lewis gun even for one night. Any one of them says no, I at least have to be allowed to ask, Corp."

"Fine." Tapscott said, "Only if you're short."

"Well," Felix looked eagerly beyond the other men, to the traverse which led directly forward, "clock's ticking; must get on."

"So, you're going, then?" Sergeant Douglas stopped him before he moved off. "If you don't, none'll think the less of you. You look tired, Catscratch."

"If anyone asks, Sarge, why I'm doing this, you can tell them I'm in it for the hours of forced rest at Company HQ before kickoff."

The lads from the section were brewing up as well, some heating water for ablutions. In the dirty daily life at the front, keeping as clean as reasonable was not only practical, but there was also the psychological perk of fresh water on rough skin. Expediency being the measure of all things done here, it was usual to go no deeper than the collar nor above the cuffs. There was little point in a body wash- even if room permitted the performance- as the clothes worn weren't getting any cleaner themselves. Shaving was also lax on the line. The expectation was that men shave daily, but a blind eye was turned every now and again. What this caused, of course, were physical accents of the experience of a front line tour. Men, who just days ago, had marched up from rest areas- where they had bathed, had a change of clothes and a return to obligatory shaving; stuffed with regular meals and time away from the shatter of the guns- would, quite possibly tomorrow, if Sergeant Douglas had assumed right, return rearward sunken eyed, dirt-smeared and bristle-chinned; stinking, tired, hungry. What little could be done to preserve cleanliness was then a key part of routine, even if it were not much more than a splash and dab that warmed the skin and pinked the cheek.

Ferguson had his day bag on his shoulder, moving in the direction opposite Felix, who caught him by the elbow as they came abreast.

"Where're you off to?"

"Regimental Aid Post for morning sick call."

"Whae's wrang wi' ya?"

"Chilblains again. That's what I get for all of that last night, frozen stiff and damp through, except now my feet are like fire."

"I need you for something. Will you be back this afternoon?"

Ferguson shrugged. "Depends on what the Surgeon says. What do you need?"

"To come with me and get the maps Collier had with him." Ferguson gently pulled his arm free, looked down at his feet and back to his friend.

"Voluntary patrol?" To which Felix nodded. "Answer's 'no'. I won't be any good to you out there with these feet. Speaking of which, I don't want to be late for sick call." He made to leave, but Felix grabbed him again, more assuredly firm than prior, which had been of chummy intent. His teeth were set.

"I don't give a toss about your feet, Fern. You are the only one who knows exactly where he is. When I said 'need', man, I meant it."

"Well, thanks very much for caring, Felix. Like it or not, I'm away to see Captain Salinger. Truth be told, you don't look all that well yourself. Come with me and let the doc check you- even just to give yourself a break." Ferguson leaned in close, as close as two heads capped with wide-brimmed helmets could, and lowered his voice. "At least, think about how you don't have to go either. Let it be someone else's turn." Felix didn't respond. He just loosened his grip and Ferguson slipped away, leaving the patrol a minority of one.

"Felix," Ferguson had turned back at the corner, "along from the wire- about twenty yards in front and fifty from the covering party's laying-up point, the ground breaks up into high furrows. One of them is deep enough to conceal a sally port, the third one along, I think. That's where he is."

"Thanks, Andy."

"Seriously, don't go. This is nothing that nobody else can't handle."

"Doesn't mean I should leave it to someone else."

"Suit yourself." And Ferguson was gone again.

Felix stepped into the fire bay, and called the men's attention. "I need volunteers for a patrol tonight." In just testing the waters of who may be keen, he was scant on the details. Pippin stuck up his hand immediately.

"No, Squeak. Not this one, it's a bit sticky. I'm looking for older hands." His eyes flitted to Brentwood and O'Leary, the other two there. Both men from the old Holding Company, they were the best bet. Their experience showed in that they had already learned, unlike Pippin, not to volunteer as blindly as that.

"Well," Felix clasped his hands in an approximation of enthusiasm which failed to clear the gate. "Who's up for it?"

"Depends on what we're doing." Brentwood countered. Now Felix would have to sell the notion of the patrol's objective as if it were the most wonderful idea ever.

"Mister Collier had some pretty important maps on him. Important enough that someone has to fetch them back."

"Who's going?" Brentwood asked in a refreshingly matter-of-fact way; not opining on the nature of the task. Felix kept his eyes to Brentwood, but could see Pippin- the school boy- had his hand up again. He was ignored.

"So far," and a trickle of a grin broke the cracked surface of a face made impassive from fatigue, "just me." Pippin's hand immediately doubled in length, it seemed, his waving a bit more frantic.

"Damn it, Squeak!" Felix hissed, "Put your poxy hand down before you signal a Zeppelin. It's still a 'no' for you."

"But, Lance Corporal-"

"No. Shut it. Well, Brent?"

"Calendar was already open, Catscratch." For crying out loud, Pippin was now waving his hand at waist level, the rest of him a coiled spring. Felix physically turned to O'Leary, for nothing more than not having to look at Pippin- who would probably be jumping up and down next. O'Leary, in the process of dealing with a frozen biscuit and a mouthful of dodgy teeth just nodded, the jowls of his pudgy face giving their assent by chain reaction. A pocket sized man, fat cheeks were compensated for by shoulders nearly as broad as he was tall. He was certainly amongst the oldest men of the platoon, but nobody was sure by what margin. His age may have had something to do about not being shipped to France with the active battalion at first. That, and he was the only private in Six Platoon who was married. Thus he was a natural curiosity to young men unfamiliar with women, even though no one could bring themselves to ask the Bulldog about it. If being without Ferguson was a deficit, the solace for Felix was that the two men he would have picked were the ones who had chosen to go. Pippin, when Felix returned to him, looked fit to burst.

"For the love of God, Squeak, it's not helping anything."

"I really need to talk to you." Came out in one rush, as if the words would disperse like mist into the cold air before they could be heard.

"There is nothing you can say that'll change my mind, end of subject." At that, Pippin did something which for him was the height of impertinence.

"But," a pause for breath, "I-"was as far as he got.

"Not interested. Why don't you get the tea out to the sentries?" Perhaps a bit crestfallen, Pippin didn't say another word and did as he was told.

"You two" Felix told his new volunteers, "stick tight here. Company HQ briefing in half an hour. Let's see who I can pull from Two Section. Back shortly." Brentwood and O'Leary both went back to their interrupted morning routine, a fresh sense of urgency in these; to beat the cold and in preparation for the night ahead. Neither men had been in a proper fight, but they had the nature of front life down pat, and more to the point, a great deal of practice in this sort of thing. Between them, they had more than a dozen patrols, and Brentwood had gone to a special school for it. O'Leary didn't have those credentials, but he was stolid and dependable. Much, though by no means all, of Felix's apprehension was allayed by getting Brent and the Bulldog to come along. To get to Two Section, Felix had to come back on himself, via platoon headquarters. Sergeant Douglas was on his own, and he called Felix over.

"Got your numbers?"

"Short one, Sarge." He thumbed to the left, "Gonna see if I can pry one loose from Tap's claws."

"Forget it." The phone rang, but stopped abruptly. The two held a moment's silence. "Aldridge took Two Section's odd numbers. With three gone from your section, I haven't enough left to spare."

"What am I to do, then?"

"I sent Nort down to Company. When he comes back, he'll look after things here. I'm your fourth man."

Chapter VII

Directly after he had indulged himself with a fortified coffee and a session of drawing, Captain McCormack put away his material to make space on his desk for the typewriter. It was a battered old thing, a travel model with quite a bit of mileage upon it. One couldn't use it at any great speed as the keys would stick, collide with each other on the way to the ribbon or misfire altogether. Fortunately, these technical faults were compensated for by the ribbon itself, being of an age where what little ink was left hardly made it to the page. All in all, it wasn't much of a mechanical convenience- not that the Captain could type all that well either. He preferred to use it to type out his orders, not from any obligation to the presentation of such things but for the very real irony of despite being accomplished at drafting, his handwriting was all but illegible. Nominally, he could have asked Corporal Cranfield, his clerk, to take dictation; but McCormack was loathe to do so. To him, it was the height of pretension to swagger about his office while someone else collected his thoughts on paper. Besides, with the way his friend Doug had told him about it, he wasn't entirely certain that this patrol was meant to be secret. Erring on the side of caution, Captain McCormack had decided that limiting knowledge and involvement to as few men as possible would be prudent. A shred of cynicism allowed him to entertain the very likely notion that Captain Lafferty had requested the patrol in the hopes of covering up an oversight to which the adjutant may be assigned blame. Of course, it was more than that; the maps left with Collier being reason enough. Friends or no, if the only concern was an attempt to save face for Lafferty, McCormack would have told him to go hang. Facts remained; those maps were out there, somewhere, upon the body of a dead officer. What Captain McCormack couldn't get his head around was how such negligence, in the taking of marked maps out of the trenches, could have come about. From what little he did know about Collier was that prior to coming up the line he had been, for months, working on the Brigade staff. Surely he must have known not to take completed maps into No-man's Land? Speculation may have been pointless, but that did nothing to quell the Captain's curiosity.

** ** ** ** **

A Canadian Medical Officer had written, year before last, a poem which had been published in *Punch* Magazine and subsequently began to generate fame, particularly in the way in which the author had described the dichotomy between life and death. Lieutenant Collier was one such who now was dead, "but short days ago"- no more than twenty-four hours- had been among those who "lived, felt dawn, saw sunset's glow." He had indeed, starting out from Brigade Headquarters at Ablain-St Nazaire along a dirt track, pitted, rutted and frozen on the bank of a sluggish river before first light. The walk, via Souchez and then taking Rue Pasteur south to where it met the rearmost positions of 16 Brigade's section of the line would, he hoped, have him at his destination before he was expected to be by his desk at eight. Despite the rough ground of the track and the dark of that indiscriminate time which could be said to be late night or early morning, Edward Collier made all haste. The sooner he could finish this, particularly if it could be done before his absence was noted, the better. The sleepless nights had become too frequent for any further delay.

** ** ** ** **

Captain McCormack couldn't remember speaking more than a few words to Collier when the latter had popped in on his way forward, which had been the only time he'd actually seen him. It was hard not to start to think about the triviality or perhaps the randomness of the present. McCormack had been in some hot spots over the course of the past five months; being shot at, shelled bombed, or just maybe the ground beneath him might swell up and atomise the immediate area, but yet, here he still was; bashing away on the heavy keys and Collier wasn't even allotted enough time at the front to have earned a full days' wage.

Sergeant Douglas shoved his head past the blanket door. "Sir?"

McCormack tapped the return bar and looked up. "Yes?'

"Tonight's patrol reporting for orders, Sir."

"Right. Come in, then, rest easy." One at a time, the four men came down the steps and took a spot in front of their Company Commander. When all were in and settled, the Captain yanked the page from the machine and began his briefing. It was always his private aspiration that he did these things right. McCormack had become an officer on the basis of his education, but by no means did he feel his military understanding was quite sufficient. That in itself was mostly self-doubt as he had done very well during those months of training before reaching the front. The other aspect was that the front was not what all those months had prepared expectations for. However, that disconnect between expectation and things as they were was a universal experience. All the old field manuals (it was the advent of war, not the removal of years from publication that made them "old") were being hastily amended to try and keep pace with the evolution of modern arms. As such, standards, which crucially unified the way of doing things, were in the process of re-evaluation. This meant that Captain McCormack had no direct reference to consult in writing patrol orders. The very best he could do was ensure as much pertinent information be given to his men as possible.

His briefing included summaries of recent reports on enemy activity. This had been minimal, with the exception of definite signs of labour in improving their defensive works. 'A' Company's raid was fully expected to focus attention, increasing the patrol's chances of remaining unseen. The Captain minced no words on the importance of avoiding detection; even to the point of abandoning the mission, while also underscoring paramount need of finding the Brigade maps. Sergeant Douglas would lead, of course, but the patrol would be reliant on Lance

Corporal Strachan on the basis of his familiarity with the ground, ergo he was to be the patrol's scout and lead guide. The two privates, Brentwood and O'Leary were two more sets of eyes at the very least, but handy if things were to go sour, hence they were patrol security. They would be leaving through one of Six Platoon's observation posts and instructed to return through another, Captain McCormack not neglecting to tell them this evening's pass. The sentry would challenge with "Sugar" to which the patrol was to give the answer "Bush." Length of night at this time of year gave a surplus of hours between dusk and dawn, but that was mitigated by a forecast of clear skies and the full moon. At nine-thirty the patrol was to be prepared to go over. With what was good circumspection by McCormack, he left it to his men to decide how best to proceed. Two things which were immoveable was 'A' Company's raid, set for eleven o'clock, and a barrage planned to cover its withdrawal at one o'clock. In which case, the patrol had best be on its way back or risk being caught under their own guns. As a caution, the shelling would be presaged by a sequence of coloured flares (red-white-red) thirty seconds before first shot. At any event, the four men were allowed until two-thirty to report back before being listed "missing."

Drawing to a close, Captain McCormack asked if there were any questions; there were none. He put the page on his desk top, relaxing his bearing just a touch.

"We will be rotating out of the line tomorrow afternoon, going directly to our rest billets. Try to make sure the four of you are with us for that. In the meantime, just relax in place, get a little sleep if you can. Rations should be up soon, so make sure to get a good meal before you go." With that, he grabbed his coffee cup and headed outside to tour his positions, leaving the men of the patrol amongst themselves.

Sergeant Douglas crested the steps of the dugout and once outside, produced his worn wooden pipe into which he then packed a pinch of shag and touched a lit match to it. Captain McCormack hadn't gone too far on his way, and he turned about, drawing himself to elbow room from the Sergeant.

"I'm not too keen on you being on this patrol, Sergeant."

"Why is that, Sir?" he asked between puffs.

"With Mr. Thorncliffe away on course, if something were to happen to you, Six Platoon would be in a sorry state. I have half a mind to order you not to go."

"If anyone were ordered to stay behind, it should be Strachan."

"I agree, but he's the only one from yesterday's patrol going out tonight. We need him. But you, Sergeant, are much more important to your platoon to risk on this caper. Why are you going?"

"Sir, my stripes don't mean a damn if I don't put myself to the same dangers as my men. How could I look young Strachan in the eye? Sir, if he insists on going out tonight- despite my advice- and he can't be ordered back, my place is with this patrol."

"And that's exactly why I'm permitting it, Sergeant. I would not have expected any less from you." McCormack turned away and resumed his trench tour.

Most of the afternoon and early evening the men spent folded into various crooks and corners of the Company dugout. They were awoken before evening stand-to by Sergeant-Major Gordon, as a visitor had come forward to see them, the chaplain, Major McCowan. So tall as to be almost required to bend double to clear the narrow entrance, the Reverend made up for it with a slenderness such that two of him could pass abreast on these stairs, and a lankiness which permanently shoved wrist beyond cuff as if his jacket had been borrowed at short notice. His head, crowned by the brimmed helmet and perched atop a telescoped neck- held in place, it seemed, by his collar of office- cast a shadow not entirely unlike that of a mushroom. Perpetually fussy, his hands were ceaselessly active. Something forgotten in his pocket, maybe; or a loose thread on a seam. A coat of dust and a squadron of flies gathered during a summer march would have him positively animated. While officers of his status were afforded a horse for route marches, Major McCowan chose to walk for two reasons. First, it allowed him to move amongst the entire battalion, at eye level, and commune with them casually. From what the men told him, he could get a good sense of morale and personal well-being. If, for instance, a man were to tell him of having some bad news from home, the Reverend could see to it to have him bumped up in the rotation for leave. The second reason why he didn't ride was that even he knew how ridiculous he looked upon a horse. Mrs. McCowan had once used the word "giraffe" to equate the image to her husband.

McCowan had come to the King's Own in a sideways fashion. From a county parish on Prince Edward Island, he volunteered immediately for the chaplaincy. While it could have been his age (somewhere on the right-hand side of "indeterminable") or his demeanour which held him back from being selected at first, it really wasn't until the Canadian Army realised- with the help of serving chaplains- that the size of the force being created was outstripping available men of holy orders. Major McCowan had been going a bit spare for anything to do before he was packed off to Ontario where he would be ministering to a newly raised Scots regiment.

It was the one thing he did exceptionally well. Personable and friendly with the men, his mannerisms became endearing; the scattered and distracted, halting speech he had conversationally was trump to the assumption of absent-mindedness. When he took to his pulpit on a Church Parade, though, his voice was sure- carrying the lesson with a powerful resonance, clear and booming in that mysterious outsized fashion of the tall and thin. His presence with the men was both constant and consistent. Nervous habits aside, when the battalion was in line, so was he. In action, he placed himself at Captain Salinger's aid post, helping the doctor as he could and ensuring the comfort of the wounded and dying. More usually he would stop by for a quick chat, a cup of tea and dole out a few sweets and tobacco before moving on. Only one cup of tea, mind, for if he were poured a second, there might be no getting rid of him, and the rank and file couldn't be comfortable using their more abrupt and expressive dialect with the reverend in earshot.

"Hello, men." He said, cheerily, pulling tins and wrapped packages of biscuits from his cavernous shoulder bag. Each man nodded in return, greeting him with "Padre", the affectionate term soldiers would use for men of his work. Reaching back into his bag, he shared out a generous number of cigarette packets, for which Felix was especially grateful. "I was having tea this afternoon with Pere Lejune," he began, the French priest who was rector of the village where the King's Own billeted when out of the line was a familiar personality to everyone in the battalion. "We had been discussing the courage men must have to perform such deeds as the one you are to accomplish this evening. As you know, he cares a great deal about you all. Let us not forget he holds us dear as defenders of his country; more particularly protectors of his village and parishioners. He asked me if I could deliver a prayer on his behalf. I was going to include it in my next service, but as I heard about your task tonight, I would like to share it with you." From his jacket pocket, he produced a few sheaves of paper, handing one out to each of them.

O'Leary squinted at his copy. "It's in French, Padre."

"Oh, yes," McCowan chuckled. "Pere Lejune doesn't write English very well."

"What's it say then?"

"Oh, dear" the Padre flustered, "let's see. It's a prayer to Saint Gertrude, of course." Lejune's rectory was named for the French abbess Gertrude who had been given an unbeatified Sainthood for faithful works in the Middle Ages. Major McCowan perched his spectacles across his narrow nose and tried his best to do Lejune's words justice. "It begins, 'Saint Gertrude, guard those of this night from the wickedness of the enemy, aid them in repulsing the interloper afflicting our country, keep them safe and alert until their return. Or such. I'm rather afraid that my French is not grand, either." He stayed with them a short while, before he left, taking a confession from O'Leary. This practice was certainly outside his wheelhouse, but there were a few Roman Catholics in the King's Own and he understood the nature of such rituals, if not the appropriate level of penance to give. He side-stepped this by asking if the man truly felt contrition and gave out one recital of the Rosary as his standard absolution. The Padre left before evening set in.

Stand-to came and went, the four men having taken their regular part at their posts. They ate together, in silence, as none of them could think of anything to say. No jokes or benign small talk could reduce that oppressive sinking feeling of imagining the probable, where trying not to think of such things only inspires the mind to make space for thinking about inevitability.

The blanket brushed aside. "Right, lads," Sergeant-Major Gordon said, "I'm here to take you out to the OP. All ready?" The patrol got to their feet. "Cups out." Gordon said, with a wink, for as each man came upstairs the Sergeant-Major poured out a heavy splash of rum. This they sank immediately, and fell in behind Gordon, weaving up and through the support line, to the firing line and along to the sap, a ditch, really, which led to their exit point, a concealed outpost some twenty yards into No-man's Land. With Douglas at the head, they would crawl forward, the Sergeant-Major shaking hands with everyone, sincerely whispering "Good luck." The same process- of handshakes and best wishes was repeated with the two men manning the OP.

Very delicately, Felix raised his head above the sandbags, moving his eyes along the horizon from left to right, impressing the panorama to mind as quickly as he could. He sank back and ran what he'd seen against memory. He caught himself nodding to his own agreement, and saved embarrassing himself by making sure Douglas thought he was signalling his preparedness to go. In that hanging moment, not unlike that of leaving the diving board with the pool all the way below, Felix held his breath and lifted himself out from the OP, sliding along in a low crawl, his mates following behind. The four of them continued forward, carefully tracing Felix's certain path until to the men left in the OP, they were swallowed by the night.

Chapter VIII

Terrific destruction over the years had transformed the land as to be otherworldly. Felix and his mates had just left planet Earth. Going over on a night patrol was something in which the individual was allowed a great deal of input, unlike a large scale event where the individual was merely strutting and fretting his hour on the stage in the hands of a distant command. The fight, in its superlative sense, was hardly a factor at this level. Whatever it was for: securing French and Belgian territory, protecting the Empire from an upstart world power or having to defend borders to the west and east as a result of supporting an ally who had picked a fight it couldn't win on its own, was right out the window on a night like this.

Occasional flares dripped in the sky, far away enough to seem very bright stars. Equally far off artillery, both the flash of the gun and the burst of shell illumed the horizon in front and behind in artificial borealis which would be quite lovely out of context. Trailing booms of shot and impact hit the ears as intermittent and distant rumbling thunder. Moving towards their goal, slowly, making their way between the cracks and fissures of the torn landscape, it was the moon, really which was worrisome. Seemingly suspended only yards aloft, full and radiant, unveiled by even a whisper of cloud, it cast wavering milky blue shadows along the tilted ground, disguising the plain and hiding the distinguishing. Stories abounded of sorties such as this where disorientation led to a terrible end- infiltrating friendly trenches in mistake of the enemy's; dropping into a fire bay, convinced it is near to home only to find oneself interrupting on the opposition; or perhaps moving unknowingly laterally, not getting any closer to anything and leaving safety further behind in an obscured and unknown direction.

Instructed to travel light, they had doffed helmets for knit caps, and opted not to wear webbing, the load bearing belt and harness for fighting equipment and other impedimenta. Tunic pockets would suffice as it was- God willing- a short out and back. Besides the ten bullets each one of them had loaded in their rifles, a five round clip was kept in both breast pockets, space being taken up in the hip pockets by the bulging shapes of a field dressing and the heavy, oblong Mills bomb they had been required to take. The only item suspended from the waist belt was the men's bayonets, except for O'Leary who had brought his trench shovel. Not that there was expectation for its use, but it was just the thing for a quick and quiet take-down. In the Bulldog's paws, such a tool was as wieldy as a butcher's blade. With less than one hundred rounds of ammunition between the four of them, they weren't perhaps a force to be reckoned with, but that was hardly the point. The whole effort would be for naught if they were forced to defend themselves. Yesterday's example of a single shot fired scuppering not only that patrol but the upcoming raid it had been scouting for was enough, at least for Felix, to keep his mind towards not being seen. They had darkened their faces and necks with char, though most of them wore scarves knotted about their collars. Bronze unit badges and brass shoulder titles had been removed, Felix actually not having replaced his from the night before. Cold at is was, the men quickly began to sweat from effort at moving unnaturally slowly and purposefully. This streaked the dark grit of char along forehead and cheeks making the effort of camouflage moot. It was widely held that boot black worked better, being by nature somewhat waterproof, but it had the effect of resembling makeup for a minstrel show and many soldiers disdained it because of the unintentional comic nature.

Having held his eyes shut, Felix opened them again, taking another look forward. Moving from point to point allowed the group to take short "listening halts." These allowed time to assess response from their movement, or any other signs of trouble as well as for maintaining bearings. Short crawls or dashes from one bit of cover to the next meant that the journey could be thought of in parcels rather than the whole distance at once. Leaving the most recent waypoint to go on, each footfall was deliberate, vision straining in the dark; flustered by the sheer impossibility of seeing three hundred and sixty degrees at all times. It was taxing enough without calculating how much farther the end was. The end could be as soon as the next deliberate footfall, the vision having missed something on the periphery while vetting what was directly forward.

"Alright?" Douglas asked, breathing the word into Felix's ear. He nodded in response, the Sergeant feeling the movement rather than seeing it. Douglas moved back down from the crest, into the dead ground behind. It wasn't that Felix was lost that was taking up time, he was dreadfully convinced he may have nodded off just then. He was equally certain to where he was. This crude hump of earth had once been a small stand of trees but could only claim burnt, fractured stumps and exposed, clotted roots. It was here that Felix had led Fern and Squeak while Atherton and Robbins had covered them from the shell hole, say, fifteen yards, slightly left. Slinking back down himself, he gathered the others around and spoke as quietly as he could.

"Next hop is to the covering point. Forward from here we'll be less than thirty yards from the wire. Hand signals only once we set off."

"And from there?" Douglas asked.

"Pretty sure I have a good notion where it is I need to go. If you could set up to give me good over-watch at the covering position I shouldn't have a problem."

Sergeant Douglas shook his head no. "You're not going out alone. Any one of us will go with you."

"Sarge, I says I'm only pretty sure I know the way. Less people tramping about up there the better. I'll take one of youse as far as the first defile Ferguson told me of."

"Fine," Douglas assented, "who?" O'Leary grunted. "Thanks, Bulldog."

Felix would wind up leaving his patrol behind him like fairy tale breadcrumbs. He put a finger up to pursed lips, shifted his Enfield to his off hand and raised himself to half height, picking his way along the scrub and fragments of the ruined copse, approaching the covering point slightly obliquely and hopefully completely unseen. Yards were feet, feet were inches, but inches were miles. It may well as have been that all existence was held within that heavy drone he couldn't figure out the source of because it was the sound of his own breathing. Infinitesimally, Felix came to the windward side of the divot, brass casings from Atherton's gun decorated the inside slopes, again relieving him of any doubt in his location. Moving in, he took up a spot whit fit quite well, being exactly where he was the night before, the ground still moulded and frozen from the long wait for the scouting party. While the others followed him in and wormed into good positions of their own, Felix once again strained into the night to gain the lay. Everything to this point, very relatively, had been the easy part. Ahead from here, any certainty was gone. As long as it wasn't his imagination, the first of those ripples Fern had mentioned was just within his eye line. Looking over his shoulder, Felix saw that O'Leary was watching him, so he chucked his head and raised his hand, palm upward just enough for the Bulldog to be able to see and set off, tenderly, a man going down a dark hallway, unsure of the breadth of the walls beyond, the final few yards before dropping O'Leary off and continuing on his own.

O'Leary shook his hand as they parted, the last of a long string of such salutations reaching back to the Company dugout all that way behind them. With a delicate manner that was sponsored by stealth, uncertainty and that ever present ripple of fear, Felix began to scratch along, over the first rise and towards the second in as low a crawl he could manage, on knees, elbows and forearm, his rifle cradled, sling wrapped around his wrist. The closer he edged along, the more work his body required to place one limb in front of the other. In an extension of time, there must have been countless, wasted moments between leaving O'Leary and where he had come to, the crest of the first rise receding into darkness, and he was utterly alone.

Distant, but carried as sound does with an eerie clarity in the dark was a slow, breezy little note, not much other than slightly forced escaping air or- Felix put a hand to where his respirator case would have been if they'd have taken them, but the sound petered. Delicate sniffs didn't tell him anything, so he put his effort back into crawling forward. There it was again, louder, closer. It was so hard to tell distance and direction. Again it stopped, Felix deciding to wait where he was until he sorted this out, dammit. Glacially, he brought his rifle from the cradle to the shoulder. Once more, the sound came; again louder, unmistakable.

"Pssst, *Kanada.*" Someone was calling him, definitely, not more than a handful of yards away, from behind a little tuft of raised earth. Felix eased the safety off.

"*Kanada,* I can see you, *kamarad.* There is no fear. Your friend; I am with him. Please, come, I will help you."

"I can see you too, Fritz." He lied. "No tricks?"

"*Nein,* ah, no. Please, we don't have much time." The safety went back on, but just for peace of mind, he slid his trench knife down his puttees, an oversize sgian dubh, and cautiously moved towards the voice. What appeared from his initial sight as a rise in the ground was in fact the periphery of a little gully furrowed by a high explosive plough as it were. Ferguson had made a good description. With now a sense of bearing and familiarity all began to seem less clothed in darkness. There were two forms by the bottom, and Felix took care coming down towards them, keeping his balance, bent kneed on a decline, just in case he needed to keep to his feet and go to his shiv. If he'd thought the patrol was a poor notion, moving towards a shadowy enemy because he had been asked nicely was being downright glaikit.

The fellow was young, perhaps younger than he, it was hard to tell. He wasn't armed, at least as far as Felix could see. The round soft forage cap topped his head instead of that bucket like helmet. He leaned as close as he dared to the ragged Scotsman.

"My officer tells me, no, told me to wait here with your man, but only an hour. We hoped you would be coming."

"Why are you here? You're not saying you want to carry him back, are you?"

"No that is too- *gefarlich*- uh, in English is-"

"Dangerous?" he posited.

"*Ja*, danger. We cannot do this. I will tell you we will take him and give him a soldier's burial. My name is Ulrich Erlenbacher, and I give you my word of honour." He thrust his hand out.

"Felix Strachan." Said he as he shook it. "I need to get his papers, his pay book, like." No sense in giving the game away now. Ulrich nodded, "*Ja*, please, take them."

Breast pockets first, Felix found the wad of folded paper, slightly damp. Sliding a hand to Collier's neck, the man's disc wasn't there.

"You take his tags?"

"What, sorry, his?"

"Tags, mate" Felix brought his own out, "did y'take them?"

Ulrich shook his head. "No. I was ordered not to touch him, only to wait." Indicating with his eye, to a lump on the ground just beyond the dead man's skyward palm. "His pistol is there." Ulrich didn't move, though he was quick to put his gaze to Felix.

"Tell ya what," Felix offered, "how about neither of us worry about that. Why don't we just leave it where it is. When I'm gone, you can keep it." He was going through the rest of the pockets, but not finding anything.

"Really? It is a very good one, I think. *Automatische Amerikaner*, yes?"

"Colt Automatic." Said Felix, almost distractedly. "A lot of officers bought them in Canada before coming over, they prefer them over the revolver. It is a very nice weapon, but let's forget it for now. Yours when I leave, right?"

"Yes, *Danke*."

"What?"

"Thank you."

"Don't mention it." As he wasn't finding anything else, in particular the usual ravage left by machine guns, he finished up. It puzzled, but for all he knew a single round had clipped him before he fell, it was far too dark and time too short to be sure of anything.

"I'm off, then." Felix announced.

"Wait, I have a pen, please, his name."

"Collier," he replied, quickly spelling it. "Edward, Second Lieutenant, Canadian."

"Yes, I have it." His hand was out again, "Best wishes, Felix."

"Best wishes, Ulrich." Again they shook, and Felix took his leave.

Chapter IX

A rough, thick forest beside a tiny rail-stop town called Petit Rejour sur Bois, Sheepy Baa Woods held the scattered ditches and scrapes of makeshift shelters and bell tents radiating outwards from the Company kitchens which was home to the majority of the King's Own out of the line. Bargain Barclay, his staff and some officers who could afford it, stayed in Petit Rejour itself. Not one ranker in the Regiment knew why they were living in a place with such a name. Those who had named it had long since moved on, in one way or another. With them had gone the memory of its actual name and thus the genesis of its nom-de-guerre. There wasn't a man in the King's Own who knew what that name was and damned few who could have pronounced it had they known.

Petit Rejour sur Bois had once had a minor function in the wool trade. Surprisingly for the alternative name given to the woods at its fringes, this function was far enough along in the process that sheep were no longer required. An old and tiny collection of stone and timber, Petit Rejour was anchored by the woods at its southern edge and by the steeple of St. Gertrude to the north. A single railway station had given it a mortgage on its industry, but that lease was not long in expiring. Increased capacity for output and Petit Rejour's inability to grow apace had relegated it to the eventuality of being absorbed by larger nearby towns as they grew outward. This process, the decline of the small for the ascendency of new methods requiring larger factories, workshops, foundries and mills had already begun, but was interrupted by the war. It would require the conclusion of this war, and the one which was to follow before Petit Rejour would become a suburb of Albain St Nazaire. In the meantime, where it was gave it a new purpose. For more than two years, soldiers had billeted within and around the town. Their own, at first; French *Chasseurs* and *Poilous* from activated local reserves. They had all gone, their presence replaced by Englishmen. Better paid and more free with their money, Petit Rejour's friendly occupation gave rise for the enterprising to connive ways of parting Tommies from their wages. War's urgency and unpredictability of direction had also seen the English fade away, an enigmatic crew filling the void they had left. Canadians. Who in Petit Rejour could say anything about that country? Permanently frozen and snow covered, wasn't it a wild land of savages and backwoodsmen? They dressed like the English- so on the surface they made it seem that little had changed, though many of these new men seemed to stop being soldiers at the depth of the thickness of their uniforms. Mind, they hadn't been near as rough and rude as expected even though the increase of manpower of the Provost detachment hadn't gone unnoticed. By and large, these foreigners were well behaved on their own parole such that strict discipline would have been redundant. Many of them could even speak French, after a fashion, or were at least willing to try. That alone raised the esteem of these new-worlders above *les Anglais*. Equally amiable was their parallel way to the English of casting money to the wind. Over the war's years, both small cafes and auberges as well as private houses with large enough parlours had reinvented themselves as Estaminets to take advantage of a growing volume of opportunity. Petit Rejour had about a half dozen of these, competing with the rest facilities provided by the army and volunteers like the Red Cross and the Sally Ann. The latter gave the more scrupulous, the teetotallers and the dangerously hung-over somewhere to be. Most preferred the estaminets for entertainment- one of them showed films- and many preferred one place over all others.

The King's Own preferred the old beer hall still placarded as *L'Oie du Nord*. Reasoning for this preference was nothing more than lazy exploration. The web of streets and lanes of Petit Rejour could be as confounding to a visitor as much as a trench system. This was the first place men of the Regiment had come upon when initially posted here. Having at hand all that was needed, the scouting parties declared the short search over at first swing, claiming the place as their own.

L'Oie du Nord was as loud as any battlefield, but the racket was all release. *Vin Ordinaire* and *oueffs et frites* could be had- at the usual premium for exchange of military scrip instead of government coins, but portions for both were generous. Song, both from the petite and rouged alto warbling old French tunes and the bawdy replacement lyrics in English from a soused chorus carried through yelled chatter, shouts for service and the popping flare of the odd fist fight. The inequity of the exchange rate could well have been a guard against smashed glass and broken chairs. For the less fickle, it was well known some of the "mam'selles" could be asked away, and with that, this estaminet had all the means to draw empty of pocket young men closer to death than they were to home.

They sang here because they had not sung on the march. No one did, really. The cheery, hat and helmet waiving claim about the extended distance from the men to a certain Irish town would be invented for the folks at home. Who would sing happy songs on the way up to the line, anyway? They certainly weren't in the mood for singing on the way back. This shift had been alright; only a handful of wounded and three dead: Those two poor fellahs from Eight Platoon who had picked the wrong time to shit and Mister Collier. Despite light losses, any time at the front was a syphon of will, and even if they'd been threatened with death to sing, it was all they could do to remember to breathe. Traffic was light in the opposite direction; a good sign that things weren't ramping up. Heavily laden men, or wagons stacked with ubiquitous crates being met coming through the rye was a sure sign that any "rest" they were moving to might not last long. Worse would be frequent sightings of groups gathered around a polished, red-tabbed crew at the roadside. When the neck was stretched with "eyes left" and "eyes right" meeting senior officers on the march from trenches to billets, it was always a bad sign. The industrial among them, within the long snake of the Regiment four abreast, could calculate the number of salutes given on the three quarter mile foot-drag, up Rue Pasteur, through Souchez to the rest area beyond Brigade Headquarters at Albain St Nazaire and form odds on whether or not the situation was about to gather steam. Along well-worn tracks, happily not interrupted more than twice by being polite to big wigs, by the time they'd arrived at Sheepy Baa Woods those astute odds-makers were satisfied that nothing was up.

This estaminet the men had repaired to was the last port of call after a long day of removing themselves from the front, and from as much of the war as possible. Marching to billets was the first, followed by showers; welcome if not altogether warm, the canvas walls of the shower tents buffeting from the blast of the super heavies by the rail yard. These guns, of immense calibre, which might fire only a handful of shots each a day were fed shells directly from the rail cars they had been brought up in. When they fired, the world seemed enveloped in the forceful shock they created. One could only imagine being underneath the result. After filing through the shower, two platoons at a time, they'd recovered their uniforms- supposedly deloused, but at least smelling a bit better- and fell in for Battalion Parade.

Colonel Sinclair had said a few, perhaps indifferent words and then released his men, within the boundaries of the billets, to their own recognisance for the next twelve hours, to fall out for pay. Here it was the men received the scrip which would be mishandled later at *L'Oie du Nord*. Two weeks' pay was signed for, less deductions. Felix himself turned ten dollars a month over to his Ma, not that she needed it, but to put it away for him. Even with allotments and separation allowance, he couldn't grasp how men like O'Leary could make ends meet for wife and children on such a pittance. If he'd put applied thought to it, the answer was the same as how his own mother managed on the stipends sent from wherever in the world his father was. At striking distance from twenty, Felix was no real stranger to alcohol. It was his pat response, in an awkwardly cynical way to the question of why he'd joined up: "The drink." It wasn't untrue, but not in the way most people took it.

Leaving Scotland behind forever, the widow Strachan had fetched up on Canadian shores with her three bairns, to be taken in by her brother-in-law who had a large hold of property close to a magnificent waterfall. Isaac Strachan had found good fortune; a cheap parcel of land paired with shrewdly bought cuttings was growing into a sharply received young label. "Inchmarlo Estates," as he'd named it had plenty of room to keep his younger brother's loves lost. Felix, his sister Morrigan and Young James, when he grew a bit, with their cousins, took school in the morning and were in the vineyards most afternoons. When the war began, Isaac's two oldest, and Morrigan's beau (a hasty marriage left unperformed) went straight away, Felix kept behind by his age. He wouldn't be old enough to go without Ma's consent for ages yet, and she wasn't about to let that happen. In the meantime, Uncle Isaac was down a great deal of helping hands, so Felix and James would have to step up.

Nineteen-fifteen came to Inchmarlo in many ways as it visited households and businesses everywhere. Alec had died at Ypres, but William was still alright, with the artillery. Morrigan's fellah nobody knew about, but she was walking out with another lad, a sailor, and that marriage went along. Isaac losing his second son phased him, much as well as he could feel for William, knowing what it was like to lose a younger brother. As that tragedy descended upon the family, it was confirmed that Ontario would be introducing prohibitive liquor laws in '16. Inchmarlo would only be able to sell for export and nobody wanted to buy Canadian wine outside of Canada. Vineyards would collapse, Isaac might even have to parcel off a few acres to compensate. Occupational obligation waning, and finally of age to do so on his own, Felix had signed on and taken the King's shilling. Now he was in France, this land of fabled wine, and he hadn't laid eyes on a single vineyard. It disappointed him a bit. After all, under "Occupation" on his attestation paper he had stated "Apprentice Vintner." Even the plonk thrown around here was miserable. *Vin Ordinaire* was just that; very ordinary. In any event, though it was less booze per volume, *L'Oie* poured a good pint of ale.

There wasn't much holding his interest here, just a handful of glasses in. His bed calling him, distantly, from a canvas coated scrape within Sheepy Baa had far greater appeal than a night's questionable entertainments. Spending fourteen day's pay in one night would make him "too weak," as it were. He was about to go.

The prevailing opinion was in direct opposition to his, judging by how packed it was. Being this crowded, Pippin had a difficult time finding his way to Felix, but the way in which he collided with the empty chair and apologised to it set the bar as to why else he might be having a difficult time. Scraping the chair away from the table just enough to give him room to plunk down, Pippin crashed into a seated position opposite Felix. The liquid left in his tall glass swished as he brought his hand to the table surface, a moist trail with a lot of spare room to work with evidenced the young lad had at least *that* much in him. He blinked at the candlelight guttering from a wick receding towards a bastion of encrusted wax around the disused cognac bottle that held it. Its dance captured Pippin's focus for a moment, before his purpose recalled him, and he moved vision from the flickering sprite to the man across from him.

"Are you minkit, Squeak?" Felix asked of him, perhaps a little minkit himself. Pippin didn't answer that directly, giving a non-committed shrug, but went right on with the pressing business he finally had a chance to breach.

"I really need to talk to you."

"This isn't about me not letting you go on that patrol last night, is it?"

Pippin's head bobbed and recovered level in that heavy way of drink where even thoughts seem liquid.

"No. The night before. I saw what happened." His attitude went from sloppily tipsy to inebriated nervousness; immediately assessing what might be beyond each of his shoulders.

"What d'you mean?"

"I couldn't hear them. They'd left me at the first rise, there, but I could still see them." He belched. "It must have been something, they were there a while, but not like they were going on about finding gaps in the wire- just crouched there at the bottom of that gulley. Mister, urm-

"Collier?"

Pippin snapped his fingers, "Yeah, him. He gets up suddenly, and he's pointing up towards the German line."

"What?"

"Pointing, like this" Pippin thrust his hand and arm outward, up swiftly, rigidly, his fist curled save for middle and index finger which were in line with the limb, thumb cocked upward.

"With his pistol?"

"Yeah. Again and again. I think they were still talking, and as he's doing all that pointing, he turns to Ferguson."

"And?"

"He's turning back, see, to face the line again, and that was it."

"What was it?"

"He was shot."

Felix sighed. "We already know that, Squeak. First time seeing someone get shot, eh? Well, it's not pleasant, is it? I wish I could tell ya you get used to it, but that hasn't happened for me yet. Try not to dwell on it."

"No!" Pippin said, with a sudden and strange emphasis, his near empty drink leaping again as he banged it on the table. "He was shot." Another belch, ruder and filthy broke surface and got in the way of his wind. "Ferguson." Was the best he could manage. His eyes rolled involuntarily, following the belch with a boozy hiccup and he vomited across the table.

Felix leapt up "For Christ's sake, Squeak!" The other man had gone over the side, taking himself and his chair slamming to the floor.

Well, Felix thought, may as just as well call it a night anyway. Bending over, he peeled the fellah from the ground and slung a limp arm across his shoulder and brought Squeak back to his feet, a strong hand steadying him with a grip on a waist belt of lengthy fold-overs still not meeting his slight girth.

Thank fuck it were Squeak to thunder in rather than the Bulldog, Douglas even; or Ferguson. Fern didn't look a big man, but he was a solid fellow. A haymaker, or some such. He would have been a heavy drag to the woods, so if it had to be done, Squeak was alright. The lad was still somewhat sensible, and participated as best he could in his own frog-march. Felix brought the door open, and the shock of the cold night washed him. What was that about Fern? Down the lane, he stopped and hoisted the sack which was Pippin more upright.

"Squeak?" That got nothing. Oh, what was his proper name?

"Phil?" Again, naught. Felix wracked his mind- he knew it started with a "P".

"Thank for not calling me Lawrence." Pippin mumbled.

"How many names do you have?"

"Only my Mum calls me 'Lawrence'."

"What do regular people call you?"

"Philip Lawrence Pippin." Came out in a gurgle.

"What about Ferguson, Phil?"

"Nobody calls me Ferguson."

"God's teeth! No, ye drunk bastard, what did you say about Ferguson?"

"Didn't say anything about him, you brought him up." Clearly there was no use in trying to further the conversation. Felix regained his grip and continued away from the raucous laughter and song of *L'Oie du Nord* to the damp stillness of Sheepy Baa Woods.

Chapter X

It was very different in South Africa, he remembered. As Captain of a Troop of Mounted Rifles, a younger Barclay Sinclair had torn across the Veldt, either on the heels of or being drawn into ambush by Boer Commandoes. He and his men slept rough most nights on a long ride; that much hadn't changed. The shift was that there was no shift. The static way this war had gone, eschewing manoeuvre for fortification, lead to all other aspects to remain stale. For more than a month, his men had called Sheepy Baa Woods their home. A soldier's capacity for adaptation, ingenuity and conniving for comfort had transformed a pastoral wood into a vagabond shelter, more like the home to Tinkers and Travellers than soldiers. Guy lines had been hung between trees, roosts for endless pairs of damp gray wool socks and the occasional lengthy strip of unwound puttees. A few bell tents stood stark white among the ash and cedar, but the growth was too thick to allow enough to put the whole battalion under canvas. Most of the men had dug little pits, just deep enough to lay in, and wrap up in blankets and tarpaulins. The farm boys and county lads certainly had an easier time of this kind of living, but by this point, even the city slickers could live rough as good as the rest. Two intersecting paths, which the men had dubbed Maple Street and Avenue Road, marked the centre point of the woods, and inwards from this cross, in all directions the forest was slowly receding as fuel for the four company kitchens and their huge sixteen gallon boilers. The smoke of wood stoves and the boilers mixed with the reek of the coal braziers, allocated at the platoon level, and the heavy dewed mist winding through the woods gave the view just beyond the edge of Avenue Road an eerily surreal quality. Figures of groups of men, just starting their day were, at this distance, spectres. Colonel Sinclair almost expected to approach such a silhouette and find it was indeed the spirit of one of his lost men.

This had been much on his mind. Yesterday, on parade, he had been presented with the results of the "long roll". Each company had called all the names of all who should have been there. Three deaths, eight wounded and fifteen sick didn't much effect that ever crucial element of effective strength which remained much as it had been on the way up to the line only a few days before. The problem was that these marginal losses were being made against an already diminished battalion. Not since the King's Own had come to France had Sinclair been able to claim a complete Order of Battle. The fighting losses last autumn had shorn a great deal from the active battalion; completely depleting the Holding Company at Shorncliffe Camp. As that hadn't topped off the missing files, each week of twenty-ish losses without an equitable arrival of new men was emaciating Sinclair's command.

The weight of that notion is what had kept him from saying much on parade. What could he say- what reassurances could he give his boys? What worth was this drudge of up-the-line, down-the-line, anyway? No one in a higher position had given him any indication of when the next show was to start, and two things bothered him about that. First was that Colonel Sinclair would have to continue to endure these trickling and inconclusive losses- and expect his men to continue to endure it as well. Second was that when- and it had to be when other than if- the Corps pressed forward, how well could he expect such a reduced level of manpower to perform? Push came to shove, he could skeletonise his Battalion Staff to provide a couple of dozen ready-made riflemen. This would mean, of course, that the functionality of the tail end, that of logistics and administration, would be just as equally depleted.

"Enjoy yourselves." He had told them, and meant it. It was anybody's guess which of the freshly washed faces would be within the crowd a week from now. He didn't say much more than his office required of him, it was becoming more than Sinclair thought he could endure and as such his capacity for cheeriness had taken the day off.

The Colonel's spirits had been bolstered slightly that evening, having called for an Officer's Smoker held in the library of Petit Rejour's Hotel du Ville, which was his Battalion Headquarters. Not only had his platoon commanders returned from course, they had brought four new Second Lieutenants with them. These young gentlemen, though never yet having a command had nevertheless also just completed this course; which had all to do with new tactical ideas at the platoon level. As he'd had to operate over a number of weeks without a full deck of subalterns, Sinclair had been forced to shuffle. Dismantling Sixteen Platoon and leaving it a notional element allowed him to move NCO's into higher positions without too much of a hiccup in the established chain of command. Some of his best platoon sergeants and a couple of the most promising corporals were elevated to Staff Sergeant and given de facto command of platoons missing officers. It was done with purpose in mind. As officers came to the Battalion, Sinclair could assign them to platoons being handled by his best NCO's. Integration, as long as the gentleman wasn't bull-headed and willing to listen and learn from experience was geared to be as smooth as could be.

Now the Officers' Mess was full again, and Sinclair was able to great his newest subalterns, hear from the returned, and begin to feel slightly jolly again. Not only did Sinclair have enough officers to fill vacancies, each of them, new and old, could impart the course material amongst the remaining platoon commanders. The Colonel was certain he'd never have opportunity again to take such time in the development of his Subalterns as he'd had with the first group appointed to the King's Own in September of the war's second year.

Later in the evening, the Brigadier popped in, a casual visit. Commanding 16 Canadian Infantry Brigade was WB Hewitt-Booth, an Englishman of that unique form of nouveau riches industrialisation had caused. The Hewitt-Booths had done quite well in textiles, owning a number of mills dotting the periphery of Manchester. Coincidentally, Brigadier Hewitt-Booth and Colonel Sinclair had done some business between their respective civil concerns. Hewitt-Booth had been perfectly comfortable in drawing half-salary in his permanent rank of Colonel, sponsoring a local Territorial Regiment, and would have expected to continue to do so if not for a need for senior officers just as pressing as all other vacancies. Never having been in field command of anything larger than a company, and that was decades gone by, WB Hewitt-Booth had his dust blown off and was handed a Brigade to work with.

Sinclair, unlike the majority of men in his Battalion, unlike the majority of the men in the CEF, had been born in Canada. Barclay Sinclair the Elder had decamped from Glasgow a young man, establishing himself very well in Toronto long before the younger Barclay came along. A part of what made him who he was, if anything, was an antipathy to "colonial treatment." He'd seen it in South Africa-British officers brow-beating the upstart Canadians with airs of superior martial knowledge. Of course, cultural superiority (presumed, that is) sometimes overlooked that many of the Dominion officers had rode rough over wide broken lands after a cunning and elusive quarry in the North West Rebellion. The Brigadier hadn't shown himself as such thus far, but Sinclair was convinced that Canadian officers should command Canadian men, at all levels. Not for any hugely nationalistic ideals, but just perhaps to prove that they were just as capable.

Hewitt-Booth was a bit difficult to figure. The hyphenated name gave prejudice that he was an upper class twit, but his speech was the truncated suffixes and broadly flat vowels of the Manchuan toiling class. Bets were on as to whether his language was affected and he was "slumming" or he was true in voice and represented the reach the lower social end could achieve in this new age. Making an assessment on where this man fit into a rigid caste system was further complicated in that through very tenuous means; ownership of coal mines which fed his factories, he had been given title as "Earl of Auginhosh." Impressive upon personal introduction, it paled in the reality that Auginhosh was a wind-swept Scots town of miner's cottages and a main road leading to the pits.

The Brigadier had been light on detail. Not for want of expression, but that he remained in the dark on anything to do with offensive planning beyond his necessity of knowledge. What he did pass along to Sinclair was a God-send. Hewitt-Booth had been assured that sufficient reinforcement would arrive to bring up his battalions' strength prior to the opening of the next battle, ideally in enough time to train them for what was coming. As to when that might be, the Brigadier could only make a vague offer.

"Not tomorrow. But any other date from now t' the Reckoning is open. We'll be wantin' good, dry weather. Springtime, perhaps. Keep your men keen, Barclay; and as safe as you can." With a tiny glass of sherry inside him-"Keeping the cold from old bones"- the Brigadier stepped on to make rounds of his other battalion camps, whisked away by a flashy motor car driven by the man who had chauffeured him at home.

The jarring wail of Reveille, played by the Battalion pipers, en masse at the junction of Maple and Avenue had carried away, much to the relief of shattered heads which had sunk a fair few the night before. Only the deaf, pure of taste or the daft racked out near the pipers. It wasn't so much the music telling the time to get up after another short night which was the annoyance, so much as it was that caterwauling they had to suffer through to get the blessed things in tune. A dentist's drill would be more welcome on a hung over morning. Already, some of the men were milling about, setting blankets out in the vain hope they'd dry, or at least not freeze, throughout the day. Little clusters gathered around the braziers, sharp coffee and sweet tea slowly joining the whiff of burning coal, crisp wood smoke, tobacco fug and the clinical itchiness seeping off the fresh layer of lime laid upon the slit latrines situated on the fringes of Sheepy Baa woods. At a wash basin stand, shirtless and shaggy haired, one of Sinclair's young men was dragging a razor over a soaped cheek which offered little resistance to the blade for lack of growth. Drawing nearer, the Colonel saw who it was, fortunate as this man was one he'd hoped to chat with on an informal morning.

"Lance Corporal Strachan," he called, and the man snapped straight. "Easy, son. You crack-to like that and you'll peel your face off with your own kit."

"Good morning, Sir."

"Good morning. Captain Lafferty tells me you managed to retrieve crucial intelligence on patrol."

"Mister Collier's maps?"

"Exactly that. I'm very pleased that you managed it so well. Dangerous work, eh?"

"No' half, Sir. We did alright. Bit of an odd thing, though."

Sinclair cocked an eyebrow, "Oh?"

"Fritz were waitin' fer us. But friendly-like."

Surprise overtook all other expression, "Indeed?"

"Yes, Sir. Just wan o' them, spoke English, yeah? Told me they'd give 'im a proper burial."

"Did he? Oh, well, you'll find that war has such saving moments of human civility. That's one for the fireside with the kids, eh, Lance Corporal?"

"God willing, Sir."

"Amen. I just wanted to tell you I'm glad I've got such men like you to work with. Major McCowan will be delighted that not only did your patrol arrive safe, but also that Mister Collier is cared for. He was quite concerned, actually."

"Was he, Sir? That's very kind. The Padre came to see us before we went off. Gave us a prayer."

"He insisted on going for a visit. Prayer to Saint Gertrude, was it? Pere Lejune has a knack for words, I daresay. I've a copy, in his own calligraphy, framed on my desk."

"Well, it worked. Can't complain about that, Sir." It was meant as matter-of-fact, but the Colonel chuckled anyway.

"How'd you come to the army, Strachan?"

"Volunteered at Niagara Camp as soon as I was old enough." He told the old lie once again. But what did it a misprinted year on his Attestation Paper matter now that he was of age? "Father's footsteps, I suppose."

"A soldier, was he?"

"Aye, Sir. A Sergeant with the Gordons." This impressed Sinclair.

"The Gordons? Very fine Regiment, Son. Was your father in South Africa, Lance Corporal?"

"Yes, Sir, he was. You might say that he's still there."

"I see. Killed in action?"

Strachan looked at the ground for a moment, as if the answer may have been printed across the toes of his boots. "No, Sir." He said, his cheeks warming from the well of distant feeling, a loss from so long ago still able to transport him standing barefoot in the back garden, the ranging slopes of peripheral Highland Albion before him; sent out in the yard by his mother who's just been delivered a letter. "He died of the fever in Paardreburg."

"I'm sorry. It's a poor death for a good soldier. Many promising men were lost to typhoid in that campaign. A real shame. I could use a man like your father."

"Thank you, Sir. I've often thought the same."

"Any letters from home recently?" he'd said in a deft change of subject, as while Strachan had imagined his youth and last days in Banchory, Sinclair heard hoof beats stirring up the dry red dirt of the Transvaal.

"Two, Sir. One from me Ma. She's worried about my younger brother, James. He'll be old enough to volunteer soon. My going was hard enough on her."

"Well, then, Strachan, that gives us more motivation to win the war so that other mother's sons aren't added to this misery. What was the other letter?"

"From my sister. She's conducting street cars, if you can believe it, Sir."

"It's a strange world this war is creating. I suppose we can only hope it's all for the better."

"Yes, Sir,"

"Anyhow, must get along. Carry on, Lance Corporal."

Felix stood there a moment, face half-shaved. He'd best hurry, as it seemed to his nose that there might be bacon afoot at the kitchen. A poor death for a good solider, Sinclair had said. That was one thing, and Felix knew that a promise of a fitting burial did nothing against the notion that Collier may not have had as fitting a death.

Chapter XI

It was far too frayed and filthy for Felix to recall whether the object he used to wipe the soap from his face was a towel he sometimes used as a scarf or the other way around. Dipping and rinsing his mess kit in the latrine's boiler, he made great bounds to Buckshee's kitchen, where a line was already forming. Bacon was one thing, but the drippings- or "dip"- was a treasured commodity. It softened hardtack to an edible consistency, equally good with bread and was ever so deliciously fatty.

Nodding to his mates as he took his place on line, Felix barely had time to settle into an anticipatory, bacon-induced reverie when someone called his name. It boomed across all other noise, projected as it was from the broad frontage of RSM Knox. A stretch of faded ribbons running from buttons to seam over his puffed breast told of a world tour without recognition for merit. The Regimental Sergeant Major had been gifted to the King's Own from a stock of retired NCO's in Britain. Knox, an upright Guardsman with an impeccable presence on parade had taken his office at Shorncliffe, setting immediately to the notion that the weeks spent before departing "Canadia" did not proper training make. He squashed their soldierly pretensions on the square until every last one of them knew their arse from elbow. He upbraided privates and officers alike, though it was unclear how much latitude Colonel Sinclair had given him for that. What he did, in that old, surreptitious way of sergeants and centurions was give the men a reliance upon one another, and most importantly – martial spirit. At the end of the day, however, he wasn't really one of them. Of all the places he had been, Canada had not been one. His own Regimental heritage insisted on him keeping to trews instead of the kilt, though he had gone so far in compromise as to have them tailored in his adopted Regiment's tartan. This pretension singled him out, even among officers enough that some joked he was there to draw fire away from the rest of them. Of those that made jokes like that, there were some who may have wished it true. Most of the men, mainly the younger ones, didn't have a vocabulary which included the word "pedantic", but had seen it defined throughout their tenure at Knox's hard school.

"What's your game, Strachan? We may be in the woods, but we're not at home to monkeys. That is a mess line, laddie. Where are you without your tunic?"

Strachan winced, his lanky arms drooping slightly, their pale contrast against his grubby singlet was evidence against himself. He'd known it was chancing it and he could be either gigged out of the line; as he now was- slinking away back to Six Platoon lines- or refused service when he got up to the cooks. A calculated risk undertaken by the importance of the objective- bacon. With that out of the way, he might as well find Squeak, who he hadn't spotted at the kitchen. Perhaps that was due to him still being inert under frosty blankets. Felix fetched his tunic and went over to kick the soles of Squeak's boots. The young man stirred.

"I feel dreadful." Which were well chosen words, matching his pallor.

"D'you want to know the trick behind not feeling dreadful after a night on the drink?"

"There's a trick?"

"Certainly. Drink less the night before."

"Doesn't really help in the meantime."

"Well, no. But feeling as you do should be reminder enough for the next time."

Pippin shifted to sit up.

"You hurry, and you might get some bacon and dip." Pippin made an involuntary noise at the notion of grease. He might puke again if he'd had anything left to give.

"No?" Felix surmised, "Either way, find your feet. First parade's in about twenty minutes."

"What's up today?"

Felix grinned. "Route march and field problems." Pippin seemed to sink further into himself. Having teased him enough, Felix took a knee next to the younger fellow and lowered his tone to something more sincere while erasing the grin.

"If you can't eat, that's fine, but try to get something in ye; for it's a lot better to have a bit of ballast. I want you to get a whole water bottle down your neck before we form up. Two, if you can."

"Thanks, Corp."

"Now," Felix continued, a further drop in volume for discretion and gravity. "Last night, you were talking about that patrol where we lost Collier." If the lad couldn't remember, Felix might be able to relegate Pippin's chat last night to nothing more than drunken hogwash, his brain having sent false reports to his mouth. That would be easier to deal with. If Squeak had not gone wide-eyed at his prompting, Felix could have- would have preferred to- remain ignorant of what might be suggested.

"Ferguson shot him."

"Are you sure? Might he have been shooting beyond the Lieutenant? Something you couldn't see from where you were?"

Pippin shook his head. "It was when Collier was pointing; he turned away. Fern, he shoulders up, takes a bead while the Sir is still looking the other way, and took his shot. Next thing, Collier's down and those flares started popping."

Felix just couldn't shake his want for doubt. "God's Truth, Phil?"

Pippin nodded. "God's Truth."

"Who else have you told about this?"

"No one."

"Right. Keep it that way. Does Fern know what you saw?"

"Don't know."

Felix rose to his feet. "Get yourself ready for parade- and not one word to anyone about this." Thank goodness his last instruction was asking Pippin to behave in his usual fashion.

"Where are you going?"

"To the Regimental Aid Post to find Ferguson."

Ferguson. Felix just couldn't fathom it. He'd known Andy from his first days in the army, they'd always been in the same section since. He was a big, tough looking bloke, but a body built by hard farm work contained a soul with little rancour. Felix could only hold Andy's recent foot problems against him, and he knew that wasn't fair. Andy was no shirker, even if his flare-ups seemed to coincide with dangerous work. He was a good friend, cheerful and generous. Part of the reason Felix had felt fed-up at *L'Oie du Nord* was he didn't have Andy to pal around with. Fern was always good for a laugh- just as quick witted if not as expressive as he, a little cynical, perhaps; but not homicidal. Squeak had either really seen what he saw, or was gravely mistaken. How well could he have seen anything? Felix hadn't found Collier until he was right on top of him, and even then had Ulrich to guide him by voice. It was true that Squeak genuinely believed what he saw, but really that was proof of nothing.

Taking Pippin's recollection of events as fact, what reason could Fern have had to kill a man he had just met in cold blood? Felix could swear that Andy didn't have it in him. Although, that was hard to disprove as he had also seen him take a man's life. Felix was no innocent himself, starting with one of the Kraut gun crew at Spoon Farm. It had been his first shot at a visible target, pleased with himself for hitting a moving object, a confirmation of a long time in practice overshadowing the morality that the object was a human being and his movement was an attempt to run, get away, keep alive. Felix had prevented this, taken away any ability or desire, permanently. Ferguson's kill, the one Felix had witnessed first-hand; while they had still been at the Somme in December, had been a great deal grittier. Andy had sunk his trench knife right the way through the back of a German who'd feigned death and tackled Felix to the ground of the trench One Section had just jumped during a raid. Large, rough hands with a fisherman's grip had found his throat, smashed away at him, and just as quickly released; the edge of Andy's blade poking through. It had cast blood onto Felix's jacket. Some spots of that encounter still remained embedded with the rest of the grot of filthy souvenirs no washing could remove. No question Ferguson had had the right of way on that occasion. Felix concluded that Ferguson had saved his life just before Christmas; or at the very least, saved him the effort of having to fight for it himself. What possibilities lay in Pippin's recollection was well beyond Felix's ken. Heading to the Aid Post to put things directly to Fern would clear the slate. Fetching up at the place, he clocked Jamieson, one of Captain Salinger's orderlies and asked for Fern.

"He ain't here. Doctor sent 'im with a couple other hobblers to Base Hospital." Those questions Felix had planned hung unanswerable, to be wiped from foremost concern by the strains of the pipers calling assembly.

** ** ** **

Captain Lafferty woke, reluctantly, from a gnawing sensation behind his eyes. It had been a night; that was sure. One of the new subalterns had been in the same house at Uni. Poor man had no idea what to expect of the front, so Lafferty stood him drinks and told tall tales. No spirit of misinformation motivated him, more so it was to put a bit of a scare into him. His most frank advice was delivered last.

"Where are you assigned?"

"Nine Platoon."

Lafferty wracked his mental file. "Staff Sergeant Belfry is your Two I/C. Stick with him and listen to what he has to say. You may be senior to him, but you don't know shit. He does."

The other fellow had just nodded, looking distracted. Lafferty could not envy him. Except perhaps now; his head being in the most awful state of affairs.

"Ugh." Was the most eloquent he could manage to the dim figure which had awoken him. "Did I eat my socks last night?"

A clipped tone answered "I have no notion of what was served at your Savage's Ball." Lafferty recognised the voice as that of Kennedy, the Brigade Major- essentially his counterpart one level up. He swung his feet to the floor, scraped a match and brought his table top lamp to flame.

"Didn't realise it was you. Sorry, Sir."

"No bother. May I sit?" Lafferty indicated the space on his cot his legs had vacated.

"Good smoker, was it?" Major Kennedy asked, Lafferty could only nod, his mouth still home to a woollen sensation. "I'm here for your Colonel. Suppose asking you if you'd seen him would be without point." This achieved another nod. "Well, I can tell you, you'll know soon enough. We're putting up another scheme."

"You're here to give orders for the 'Big One'?" Lafferty asked.

"No, no. Biggest one so far, though. The whole Division on a Raid. Set for three weeks from now. Dress rehearsal, I'd wager."

"Makes sense." Said Lafferty, who despite his garish state was able to hear the penny drop. Of late, all patrols and raids had moved from small affairs to whole companies, battalions and brigades. A division raid presaged a corps attack, which could only be the big show.

"Your battalion will be setting up a blocking position to protect the left edge of the raid area."

"Get to shake out some of the new bugs." The Captain said with a mind to the young man he had cautioned the night before.

"True." They both nodded. Lafferty pointed to the back end of the loft.

"Colonel's Roost that way, Sir."

Kennedy stood. "Ta."

"Oh," Lafferty added before the Major could leave. "I've got those maps to give back to you." He pulled them from the table drawer and offered them to Kennedy.

"What maps?"

"Those ones that went missing; those Collier had taken with him. These maps. We got them back."

"First I'm hearing of it. Who's Collier?"

"Young second looey, Brigade Headquarters; came up the line on a transfer couple of days ago. You're saying Brigade isn't missing any maps?

"If any maps leave HQ, they have to be signed for. Those chits wind up on my desk, and I've not seen one. Fact is, our map section is busy with some sort of arts and crafts project; large scale reliefs of the Ridge. I don't recall any officers transferring out and no one named Collier at all. We do have a missing officer, with the Provost. Lieutenant Osgoode, failed to report one morning."

"Doesn't ring a bell."

Kennedy shrugged. No sense dwelling in the unknown- too much of that about lately. He had two other battalion CO's to brief which would include going over a complex schedule of stringent work-up training from today's date forward to zero hour. It was a juggling act. Kennedy had to allot three battalions time in a training area only big enough for one at a time, while also keeping regular trench rotations in effect in such a fashion as to have the entire Brigade fit and ready for their assigned tasks in less than twenty-one days. It was this that demanded his closest attention. A man dropping off the face of the earth was too common an occurrence to pay it much mind, and as such failed to register as an issue altogether.

Major Kennedy left Lafferty still holding the matted wad of what had once been of critical value.

Lafferty turned them over in his hands under the lamp. They were still soggy, clotted with blood, runny ink passing through the layered folds. He had not closely examined them before, realising they'd become quite fragile. He'd thought getting them back to Brigade might mean the map boys could restore or recover the information. Didn't seem to matter now. Gently peeling at a free corner only came away with small, pulpy chunks. Whatever these things had been, they were now devoid of any purpose. He let them fall into the waste bin, where they landed with a squishy thud. Lafferty's ire rose in return. That lump of crumpled papers had cost a life and their retrieval- thank goodness for good endings- had put four others at risk of theirs. For nothing at all. Just who the Hell was Collier, anyway?

Chapter XII

France, March, 1917.

A sizzling whip crack sensation inches from his head left his right ear ringing, and inspired Felix to keep his chin to his chest, causing him to wonder if it were possible to reduce his profile enough to hide behind the brim of his helmet.

"Movement on the left!" someone called. The counter attack they had been expecting was upon them. Thorncliffe got a Very light ready, and ordered his platoon to "Watch and shoot!"

"At what?" McCallum asked, earnestly.

"Muzzle flashes." Felix told him, no fault in his not knowing; having only just joined the platoon last week. Sure enough, there they were in the blue-black dawn, in twos and threes, little colonies of fireflies followed by the short sharp bark of the report, itself heralded by the snap of lead tearing the air overhead. As long as they went "zip!" it was alright. It was when they went "thud!" which was worrisome. Six Platoon's return fire, aimed and deliberate, seemed to check the enemy's approach.

The Germans had obliged them by advancing from where they had been expected, across a stretch of ruined trenches. Abandoned months before while tightening defences elsewhere along the line, weather and shelling had pummeled it to a mere rip in the ground. Through a defile, these grey wraiths picked their way towards the hasty redoubt "B" Company had thrown up as a block against them. While they were where they had been expected, they were later and fewer, thinly spread in small groups-uncharacteristically disorganised.

The gas had helped. Cylinders along the whole Division front, two thousand yards wide, had been opened at three o'clock. At this stage of things, gas was no real surprise or terror. So quickly had it become part of the war, its use and defence against it was routine. Its effect, if not in causing casualties, forced those nearby to continue to work and fight wearing claustrophobic and sensory limiting respirators. The rolling blooms of rusty haze settled in low areas and had made the counter attack route for the Germans treacherous to cross. These forces had been held back at rallying points; patrols sent forward reporting a second, but lighter burst of gas two hours after the first. They stayed put, to wait it out in a small clearing on the leeward side of their lines. It was one of a handful of such concentration points the Flying Corps had identified and given to the artillery as part of the day's fire plan. This was led by an isolating barrage of the raid's periphery, boxing the area with a shroud of high explosive. Flinging thirty-five pound shells of shattering menace, the howitzers broke fast just before six, long before sunrise. Held firm by the threat of the gas, German marshalling yards were obliterated at a heavy toll. Joining in a few moments later, the lighter 18 pounder field guns- one for every thirty yards of front- threw forward shrapnel shells, gunners rhythmic in their drill; apace for four rounds a minute. Each gun commander had a precise timetable of when and where to change the gun's elevation. In synchronicity, the 18 pounders created a moveable wall of whirring and bursting lead bearings the raiders could confidentially walk behind. The counter attack worming towards Six Platoon had already kept alert for nearly three hours, most of it wearing masks and then had been shattered by the covering barrage. Still, they had come, a trickle more than a rush, prodded on by the NCO's and officers who remained.

Thorncliffe moved up to the lip of the crater, its edge given a quick dressing of half-filled sandbags- a

few had jagged rents across them. Six Platoon held
the leading point of a series of impressions left by
terrific explosions. Some time ago, five mines had
been blown- by one side or another in a mutual
attempt to collapse underground shafts. From a
view no one on the ground could see was a sequence
of holes as a slightly avian shape dominating two
smaller, separate ovals. This feature was well known
as Gosse Egg Craters. Eight Platoon had taken the
two "eggs", stringing loose strands of barbwire
between its sections' posts. Seven Platoon tied in
with Eight between another hasty wire obstacle, at
the bottom end of "the Goose" itself, Five Platoon had
been relegated to Company Reserve and formed up
around Captain McCormack's command at the
centre of the bird. When the artillery had opened up,
the men of Buckshee had set out to take possession
of the craters, and prepared to defend them for the
hour or so the raid would be in place. Shifting earth
and bags to grant a bit more cover, they had waited
to be met, the crash of the big guns echoing
throughout.

Gas and shell had interrupted the usual
punctuality of the Germans, though now that they
had decided to come on, it might not be long before
the fierce, rolling momentum they were feared for

was gained. Little could stand in the path of the violent havoc the *sturm* might gather. While it seemed that the Canadians had gained the advantage this morning, things had not gone without a hitch. The worst of these was that the Vickers machine gun attached to Buckshee Company had yet to arrive. While they had all started off together, Sergeant Stewart and his crew had set up on an intermediary point to give covering fire on the Company's surge towards Goose Egg Craters. When the Company was in place, Stewart was to move and mount his gun at the Craters. No one from his team had made it. Thorncliffe had been about to send a runner to try and find them, but the Germans had interrupted that notion. Certainly the counter attack was weaker than expected, haphazardly disjointed, rapid rifle fire and the Lewis gun seemed to be sufficient to hold the enemy in place. The absence of the Vickers, though, had robbed them of a tremendous amount of firing power, to a level of deterring any encroachment from the busted defile. A problem with the Vickers was its weight. The gun, tripod, water can and ammunition required a team of porters to handle. In static positions little rivalled the deterring suppression this gun was capable of. Its robust weight was accounted for in solidly built moving parts, as well as several gallons of water, evaporated and condensed within a jacket shrouding the barrel which kept the weapon cool enough for lengths of sustained firing, but didn't do any favours for mobility. The Lewis gun had been a good compromise offering much more portable fire support, but as it was air cooled and magazine fed, it couldn't maintain the same discouraging rate of fire. This was why Thorncliffe had moved to the crater's edge, to check in with Atherton on the Platoon's Lewis.

"Doin' what we can, Sir." He told his officer between bursts.

"How's your ammo holding?"

"Few pans, ten, maybe."

"Start refilling from your bandoliers, I'll send someone to beg a few pans from Five Platoon. Keep your rate as high as you can." Atherton and Robbins continued while Corporal Tapscott organised the rest of the section in peeling .303 rounds off the metal clips of five they were delivered in and snapping them, as quickly as cold, nervous hands could into the empty flat drums which fed the Lewis. Besides the heavy machine gun which by all rights should have been in this position, Thorncliffe was also without rifle grenades.

When he had returned from course last month, he'd been able to re-form his platoon in a dynamic new format. No longer standard was the platoon of four equal sections of riflemen. The need- or more succinctly, the critical necessity- to match the strength of enemy positions inspired the notion to specialise each section within a platoon to a particular function. It was a promising idea. The Lewis Section could provide covering fire on the advance no rifle section alone could achieve. This would permit the Rifle and Bombing Sections to close with the enemy and turn him out with bayonet and grenades, while the Rifle Bomb Section would lob their wares onto strong points and rifle pits as miniaturised mobile artillery. Six Platoon had spent the majority of the past three weeks- in between regular front line rotations- working on these changes and incorporating them in preparation for this raid. While the men seemed to adjust well and the whole idea brimmed with potential, the special equipment needed to allow a Lee-Enfield to fire a rifle bomb was still in too short a supply to issue. There was not enough time to get everyone familiar with it, so for this morning, Three Section was only with their rifles, a logistical logjam having defanged them. In turn, this made the absence of a machine gun even worse. Thorncliffe was going to move along- to check in with his other sections- and asked Atherton in parting "Need anything else?"

The gunner looked at the Lieutenant's left hand, at the flare gun. "A little light would be grand, Sir."

"No problem." Thorncliffe smirked, bringing the Very pistol to bear at an angle between horizon and canopy. Pulling the trigger made a funny, hollow sound; such as a cork rapidly escaping a bottleneck which was shortly followed by a puff and an instant bath of shimmering light. At once, Six Platoon's fire increased, picking out targets they could now see, but only as long as the flare was aloft. Germans scrabbled like ants to find folds and shadows to hide in. Both Atherton and Thorncliffe were smiling now, their work for the next few seconds made all the easier.

It cut both ways. The forward lines of German trenches, those that the counter attack defile interrupted, took advantage of the light and opened up with raking fire on the Goose Egg. It also caught Sergeant Stewart's crew, who were strung out in a long line, burdened liked Sherpa, facing the wrong direction.

The flare pointed out their error, but exposed them to the Germans on the heights. Before Stewart could rally his men to head the right way, a hurried fusillade was sent out at them, scattering men and the kit they carried. Coming to rest on the ground, the flare guttered and blinked, leaving darkness. Firing on both sides checked pace slightly, but didn't stop on account of the flare dimming. Particular attention was being given to the locale where the machine gun team had been caught in the open. Thorncliffe reacted, wheeling to Corporal Norton's One Section.

"Fetch that gun in!"

Between the shelter of the crater and the harried gunners lay only a handful of yards. Norton pushed himself up, his left foot swung out to start a sprint that never happened; a hard smack knocked his head aside and blew a jagged pair of holes in his steel hat, felling him in one movement back to the ground quicker than he had risen. The rest of the men balked, McCallum especially, as he was already quite clueless and frightened and now his eyes were wide, stark white against his broad cheeks smeared with the patina of what had been on the inside of Norton's head.

"Catscratch!" called Thorncliffe. "Don't let those bastards take that gun!"

Well, Strachan thought, if he was going to die, so much the better to have it happen doing something constructive rather than lying there waiting for it. McCallum was quite useless, his mind refusing to comprehend what was happening; locking itself down in the numbing protection of shock. Felix took his rifle from him and charged Squeak to mind him.

"Stay here, keep him down- don't let him wander." He instructed. Squeak nodded enthusiastically, quickly embracing McCallum, who offered no resistance and brought him to ground. Felix shouted over to Atherton.

"See us there safely, will you?"

"I'll do my best," was his reply while swinging his weapon on the axis of its bipod to bring the muzzle toward the heights. Robbins slapped a new pannier tapping Atherton on the shoulder, who immediately got on with his job. At least the ripping burp of the Lewis was drowning out the sound of Mauser rifles, except for the startling whine of near misses; nothing silenced that.

Drawing up O'Leary, Brentwood, Taverly and Edward by eye, Felix led them out at a run so fast he wasn't sure that he touched the ground between the crater and the stranded gunners. O'Leary was with him, Taverly right behind, sliding in like stealing third. The other two had gone down, but Felix hadn't seen it. The Vickers was scattered where the crew had dropped the parts when they had gone for cover. Sergeant Stewart was dead, both he and one of his ammo bearers perforated by that opportune hail of gunshot. The bearer's boxes had spilled their contents, surrounding the two bodies with brass cartridges like a lost treasure. All else was inert behind what little bumps and rises to be taken to, held there by sporadic fire from several directions.

Felix put his boot to the first arse he came across. "The Hell are you doing? Get up from there and get your gun working, for Christ's sake-you too!" he shouted at another cowed gunner. "You're no good down there. Show these bastards what you're made of! Bulldog, Tav, with me, covering fire while they work." He pointed to the rise off to the right, where the twinkle of flashes was most thick. "You, there," he said to the gunner under his boot, "I want your fire along that spur in ten fucking seconds!"

"But we ain't got the tripod," the man protested. Felix grabbed the bearer's body, wrestled it in place against a hummock, giving enough surface to rest the gun and elevate point of fire.

"There. He's useful again. Get that gun working with that and I'll get your bloody tripod." Felix began his count to ten, to himself, even if he didn't have a follow up if the gunners failed to perform. In the meantime, he fired his rifle and flicked the bolt hurriedly while the men fussed with the Vickers, which didn't seem to be going well. The nearest belt was in a tangle, one of the gunners frantic in finding the leading end while the other rather timidly attempted to brace the gun between the berm and the dead bearer. Felix and his section were firing as fast as they could, but rifle fire alone couldn't pin down the Germans raking them with fire from the heights. Each shot splattered the ground in a way that created grey hairs; a little puff of dirt the only tell-tale of lead moving faster than they eye could see. Before Felix had reached ten, without so much as a cough from the Vickers, O'Leary intervened. Chucking his rifle at the fellow trying to sort the belt, he pointed at the German works, said "There!" and yanked the canvas belt free. He leapt at the other man, taking up the gun in his brawn, putting his mass behind dropping it down. Reaching up, he caught the gunner by the lapel and threw him over the barrel's water jacket, "Stay!" being his instruction to a living counterweight. Deftly, O'Leary ran the leading tab through the feed box, drew back the charging handle twice, thumbed the trigger and was rewarded with a generous burst that chewed into the German parapet, jostling the young man over the barrel.

"Tripod, Catscratch!" O'Leary shouted above the rhythmic thump-thump-thump of the Vickers. Felix didn't know quite why he had volunteered himself for that caper. Laying splayed out- it had been carried in its open position- the pod lay a half dozen yards away; immobile humps of the others of the gun crew surrounding it. Slanting his helmet as if to walk out into a drenching rain he said "Be right back," then, "don't slack off that fire, Bulldog", who may or may not have grunted in response. Once Felix rose up, it became as if he was the only person on the battlefield. Bullets sung past his ears as on a summer evening alive with mosquitoes and pecked dirty little fountains at his feet. He made it, breathless, to find of the two men around the tripod, only one was wounded, Corporal Brimley, who's right hand had been smashed by a bullet, his fingers sickly askew. The other had just not gotten up after having been shot at. He had used the water can as something to hide behind, but the holes through its skin disproved its usefulness for that purpose and rendered it useless for the one it was intended.

"Alright, Corp? Felix asked.

"My hand's a bit fucked."

"I see that. Fair nasty. Eh, no sense in sticking aroon' here- we've got a much nicer spot over yon" he chucked his head. "What d'ye say?"

Brimley nodded in agreement. "Shaughnessy, on that tripod, we're moving." Shaughnessy came into action, picking up his equipment, including the punctured water can, and attempted to shoulder the fifty pound tripod. Felix slapped the dribbling tin can from Shaughnessy's grip.

"You don't need that," he said, while feeding stripper clips to top up his magazine. He crouched down, as small as he could behind a single, runty tree stump; the only probable bullet stopper to hand, and slammed closed the bolt.

"When I say, go like stink to the gun pit. One bound, stop for nothing."

"What're you gonna do?"

"Provide you cover. Do me a favour and turn that aroon' when it's my turn to come across?"

"You got it."

Felix rolled into as good a firing position as he could manage. "Go!" he shouted, quickly firing twice, adding marginally to O'Leary's output on the Vickers. Brimley and Shaughnessy dashed over the open ground, though there now was less to bother them on the way. Once there, the gunners seemed to swarm around O'Leary and when they parted revealed an assembled and stable gun. Shaughnessy now took the triggers, more expertly landing his shots and chancing longer bursts. German fire receded to near nothing. Felix could have danced his way back unmolested, though running full tilt was decidedly more prudent.

"We're going to need water" was Brimley's concern. Felix handed him his own bottle.

"How long can you keep firing when the water runs out?"

"Not long, not at a good rate, anyway. How much longer are we here?"

"Half an hour, a little more."

"It'll be a near run thing."

"I'll get everyone else's bottles, then."

"Good. Let's keep the rifle fire up, too."

"Right." Felix agreed, crabbing his way from man to man, lifting their water bottles and tossing them towards Shaughnessy; one of his mates transferring the liquid to the weapon's cooling jacket, great geysers of steam being released in the process. Without the condensing hose and the water can to collect it, in due course all of it would evaporate and the gun would soon overheat. A lone figure popped up from the Goose to sprint over to them. It was Dewey, one of Six Platoon's runners, coming to give a message to Felix.

"Hiya, Catscratch." Dewey said, the rarest of personalities; that of boundless enthusiasm unperturbed by chaos ruling around him. It was as if he'd come over to borrow a cup of sugar.

"Dewey." Felix acknowledged.

"Mister Thorncliffe says to hold your position here and keep your fire on the high ground. Signal to withdraw is one long and three short on the whistle. Your squad will move first. Leave the dead."

"Okay. Tell the Sir we're good to go, but I'm going to need you to come back here with as many water bottles you can carry."

"My pleasure." Dewey beamed and set off. Felix breathed a heavy sigh. Just a little while longer and they could pack it in. His ears picked up in anticipation of Thorncliffe's whistle piercing the thrum of the Vickers and the punctuated cracks of rifle shots.

Chapter XIII

Another wave of aeroplanes silhouetted against a sparkling sky passed overhead the men reposed on a little hill.

"How many is that?" Asked Brentwood. Felix squinted at the midday sun.

"Don't know. Quite busy, though." It was. They'd only been resting here for less than an hour and several echelons had come and gone, always in small groups and disappearing long before the rumbling chop of their engines receded.

"What d'you suppose they're up to?" Brentwood seemed inquisitive today, more musing than demanding information.

"Taking pictures, I imagine. How else do you think those models came to be?"

Brentwood seemed satisfied by that. They had all just recently been sent to see the sand tables- relief maps- which were built for the upcoming attack. It was impressive, in scale as well as detail. Not only did the Ridge climb up almost to a man's height, every crease and fold had been meticulously recreated. Even without labels, the men of the King's Own could easily pick out familiar spots as they had been herded by the model. There was Goose Egg Craters, where they'd been fighting just days ago; and just down from that was the re-entrant of the German line their front-line positions faced. It had been labelled "Castle Switch" and few among them had any doubt of what they would be asked to do.

In battle, the infantry has one role- to close with and destroy the enemy. The first part, the closing, is performed by a technique known as "fire and movement" in which the enemy is constantly kept under fire while men can move forward in short bounds. It is winning the firefight that enables the infantry to move to "closing distance" from the enemy where the assault to destroy him will be carried out. Use of "fire and movement" is just a means to an end and it might even seem deceptively simple, but as the two tasks are undertaken concurrently, in reality this is a very complex notion which requires-has always required- a great deal of control and coordination. Such control can only be gained through training and repetitive drills. With insufficient grounding in the fundamentals the likelihood of a successful infantry attack are greatly diminished. The advantages of the enemy's strong defenses meant that the crucial first step of the attack, the closing, was far more difficult to achieve, almost to a point of futility during the war. Surmounting this dilemma was only possible when infantry platoons had become better armed. Introduction of effective hand grenades and especially the Lewis light machine gun gave a comparative level of firepower against well-defended positions; the forty men or so of a platoon could deliver more firepower than the erstwhile rifle company could. The tactics developed around these weapons were more a modification of existing notions than anything entirely new. It was just new on such a smaller level.

Brentwood had only just come back from hospital and was still a bit ginger in sitting. Right now, he lay on his side, a folded blanket under his rump, protecting his delicate end. On the run to get at the Vickers, a German bullet had creased Brentwood's backside. He'd been lucky. It was a graze rather than a through shot, providing mirth and embarrassment rather than serious injury. Edward had been less fortunate, and was to be counted with Corporal Norton as One Section's dead. Young McCallum had been quietly packed off to one of those new wards, those kept separate from others at

Base Hospitals. No one anticipated his return. Not many of these nervous cases were returned to the front line.

Last year, when he had been up at Wimereaux getting a needle thin shell splinter pulled from his shoulder, Felix had chanced upon what was known as the "NYD" Ward- "Not Yet Diagnosed." The patients were in varying states of distress, wandering gormlessly, raving or staring blankly at things they couldn't see. It was bone-chilling to see men so damaged; not for their frighteningly erratic behaviour, but for the very prescient idea that this kind of collapse could be anyone's fate; his fate. As it was, what happened on the journey back from the hospital to his unit proved to distract his thoughts on such matters.

"Do you not fancy that?" Brentwood started up again.

"What, flying? No, thanks."

"Why not?"

"Too bloody dangerous." Felix explained, lighting a smoke.

"We're not exactly serving tea to grannies in our day-to-day, Catscratch."

"Good point," he acceded, "I'll sign up for the Flying Corps tomorrow."

"You won't." Brentwood stated.

"No, I won't, Brent. Someone needs to stick here to make sure you don't get yourself killed. I'd wager the fellah what pinked you wouldn't miss twice, given the chance. I wouldn't." The other lads chuckled a bit, but there was a heavy truth within Felix's joke. Now that Corporal Norton had been killed, Felix had been bumped up to command One Section. The first difficulty in his new appointment was that he had little grasp on what he was doing. The next was the challenge of not letting on that he didn't know. Finally, and by far the worst was the stark realisation that as One Section's Commander, he was directly in line behind Lieutenant Thorncliffe and Sergeant Douglas in Six Platoon's chain of command. Something were to happen to both the Sir and the Sarge and Felix would inherit the platoon. That eventuality bared no deep thought, as if he felt out of depth where he was at now, well, he'd fuck it up, for sure.

Felix only having a slim notion of his new job, at least he had only a slim notion of a section to cut his teeth on. Five of them, himself, O'Leary, Brentwood, Pippin and Taverly were fit- and Brent had only just come back. Besides the dead and the invalided from Goose Egg Craters, Ferguson had been gone since

Doctor Salinger had sent his foot cases to hospital in February. All that did for Felix was leave hanging his curiosity. Squeak had, as far as he knew, lived up to his pledge of silence; but a part of Felix worried that keeping this secret was more about protecting a friend rather than waiting to sort out facts. Nothing wrong with that, at face value; he dearly held the ideal of loyalty to friends. Just when, precisely, was it more right to put loyalties aside in interest of morality? Felix was no philosopher, and in that case, was glad for Squeak's ability to remain quiet. Having such implications come to light was something Felix would rather not happen until he knew what the right thing to do was. He certainly didn't have any further clarity now any more so than when Pippin had first confided in him, so he just tried not to think about it. More and more, Felix's mental world consisted of things rather not thought about. Fortunately, there hadn't been too much idle time between then and now, first in training for the Goose Egg, that day itself, and now the earnest work from the coming battle. When not in the line- and they hadn't been since being relieved the day after the raid- every waking moment was spent running up and down a nearby hill used as a surrogate Ridge; going through the precise actions they would perform on the Big Day. Only in the short breaks they had in between their mock attacks did Felix' mind wander. The lads' idle chatter helped to push errant thoughts aside. These days, it wasn't the implication of Ferguson shooting Collier so much as how his mind was drawn to his kilt. Since coming off the line after Goose Egg Craters, much of his time was spent musing over the small collection of holes it had seemed to gather. Being the finest garment he owned (although, in strictest technicality, he didn't *actually* own it; the King did), the idea of moths getting at it distressed him a great deal. Felix wasn't sure when precisely the correct conclusion dawned upon him, but when he did, he could think of little else. One of the tears was very close to the apex of his legs, just below his apron pooch and shockingly close to a wound no man wanted above all others.

Squeak said something, and as usual, the first attempt was drowned out by the wind.

"What, Squeak?"

"I said 'Here comes the Sarge.'" There was a collective groan. Douglas was indeed upon them, but motioned for the men to stay relaxed with one hand, his other held a collection of papers and envelopes.

"I just wanted to be the first," he began, "to welcome Catscratch and the Bulldog to the Club."

"Eh?" said Felix.   Douglas thumbed the blue, white and red ribbon on his chest.

"This Club. Both Thorncliffe and the Captain put you in. Seems that effort you put in the other day is worth the Military Medal. Well done, both of you."

Felix was floored, O'Leary inscrutable.

"There'll be a bit of a paper shuffle, but it should be official in a few days. Just try to look surprised when Bargain Barclay tells you about it." Handshakes and back slaps were given all around.

"What about Tav, Sarge?" Felix asked, "He was right there with the Bulldog and me."

"Sorry. Only the two of you got the nod."

"Oh, Hell. Bad luck, Tav."

Taverly wasn't perturbed.   "No never mind, Catscratch. It was youse what done the heavy work. I didn't do anything grand."

"Palaver. I was glad to have you there with us."

Tav blushed a bit. "Thanks."

"I mean it," a cheeky grin broke free. "Far better than Brent just sitting on his arse back there."

"No fair!" Brentwood protested. "I was shot in that arse."

"You were shot <u>across</u> the arse. There's a difference."

"Still hurts."

"Are you finished?" Douglas asked, slightly irritated. "Right. We're going to run through another attack in ten minutes' time."

"When's lunch, Sarge?"

"When they tell me, Brent. Oh, but that reminds me, Catscratch, after lunch you're to report to Battalion Transport. A whole bunch of youse are going up the Division School."

"For what?"

"To learn how to do your new job. Christ knows you're not bright enough to figure it out on your own." As a gibe, it cut a bit close such that Felix fought not to let it show. "Here's your section's mail." He handed the envelopes over and parted.

Felix gave out the letters, thankful that Douglas hadn't included any post for the lost men; he wouldn't have known what to do with them. He tore open the envelope addressed to him, quickly glancing over the template script of his mother's handwriting. His eyes stuck on a sentence halfway down the page. Blinking in the bright sun, he read it again; allowing Ma's words to sink in.

"Aw, fuck!" He exclaimed.

"Something wrong, Catscratch?"

"He took the train to Toronto without her knowing. He's joined up, the fool."

"Who?"

"My brother. Silly bugger just couldn't wait to go for a soldier."

"How's that any different from any of us; from you, Felix?"

"Because he's my wee bra'r and should be at home with Ma."

"That could be said of all of us. I'd rather be at home with your Mum than here in France."

"Careful how you speak of me Ma, Brent." Felix said through bared teeth.

Brentwood put a stopping palm up. "Didn't mean it like that." Felix recanted his hostile look.

"Sorry. I guess I had hoped to spare James all of this. There's no adventure to be had; but he'll be finding that out soon enough."

"Could end before he comes across the pond."

Felix was beyond help in not putting that wishful thinking to scorn.

"You see this ending any time soon? This is the Reckoning, Brent. Miles to go before we're done with it."

"That's a cheery thought."

*** *** ***

Colonel Sinclair was having a similar angst with the written word. Captain Lafferty's daily reports, which he'd just delivered, had included congratulatory messages from the Corps and Division Commanders on the success of the raid. Not to be outdone, Brigadier Hewitt-Booth had added his own.

"In keeping," it began, "with the praise my Headquarters has received from the General Officers Commanding the Fourth Division and the Canadian Corps, I too wish to acknowledge the fine display of arms this Brigade's battalions put on in assisting the raid of First March." It was all very kind, but these adulations had been delivered with his Adjutant's most up-to-date strength return.

"God damn these raids, Jock." Sinclair snapped with the freshly read reports now limp in his fist to the only other man nearby.

"Eh, uhm, I don't know about that, Barclay." Was Major McCowan's response, treading lightly on the Colonel's blasphemy.

"Honestly. I get new chaps, have time to work them in and we get clipped on a piecemeal action while we still have to get up that bloody thing in front of us."

"We'll get more men."

"From where, Jock?"

McCowan's mind reset to default. "The Lord will provide, Sir."

The Colonel turned sharply. "Will He, Padre?"

This made the Chaplain have to explain his ecumenical belief to the tune of Sinclair's lapse of faith.

"Who else could?"

Chapter XIV

For the tenth, or perhaps twentieth time, Felix brought his medal from his tunic pocket and turned it over in his hands. Its weight in silver alone gave it precedence as the most valuable item he had ever possessed. Just this morning, he'd been sent from the school- his second day on course- to form up with his Regiment for a Brigade inspection by the G o C of their Division. He and O'Leary were given their decorations in a plush box, the General pinning the representative ribbon on their tunics himself. After dismissal, the men moved off for a day of sports, and Felix made his way back, with Ellins from Two Section to one of the new camps which had popped up recently. The two of them would have to stay late in class today for the lessons missed in the morning.

"Do you know what Napoleon said about such things?" Ellins asked as they tramped, abreast, down the corduroy road leading to their temporary accommodations. Felix put his prize back into his pocket.

"No. Something French, I'd imagine."

"He said 'a soldier will fight long and hard for a bit of coloured ribbon.'" Felix didn't quite know what to make of that. He was personally convinced the reward for his actions wasn't the ends he sought. Thorncliffe had asked him to do something, and he had done his best to do it. What was certain was this recognition, in eighteen months of army life, was beyond anything his father had had earned in his decades long career. From what he did know, Da was no slouch; he'd seen his share of fighting in Colonial campaigns. Felix's middle name was "Dargai", which made son a memento of one of his father's battles. He'd not told his mother about his medal, despite the pride he felt, a vindication of sorts, because he was certain it would only cause her worry. She'd enough to prey on her mind now, thanks to James.

Felix had gone so far as to see the Padre about it, at lunch the same day as Ma's letter arrived.

"I don't understand, Felix." Major McCowan had said. "What is it you wish me to do?"

"Get him excused."

"Ah. Is your family under hardship with both of you in the army?" The sprawling acreage of Inchmarlo Estates came to the young man's mind. His family was not wealthy by a great stretch, but they wanted naught. It didn't seem right to lie to a Chaplain.

"No, Sir."

"Not much I can do, I'm afraid. I admire your concern for your brother. It shows you embody His teachings. Pray for James' protection."

"That's it, Padre?"

"It's really all you can do, Son. Leave what you cannot do with God Almighty. Meanwhile, put your desire to protect others with your men. They, for the time being are all your brother."

Felix had had to leave as per Sergeant Douglas' instructions to join the NCO's course.

"Thanks, Padre."

"Go with God, Felix."

They were staying at a camp called "Moose Jaw", which Felix found odd.

"What the Hell kind of a name is 'Moose Jaw'?" He'd asked Ellins when they'd arrived day before last; a placard at the camp's boundary announcing the name of their temporary home.

"It's a town in Saskatchewan," the other answered without hesitation.

"Oh," Felix had said, "but I still think it's a fairly daft name."

Ellins, who was from Medicine Hat, shot across the bow with "Why don't you tell someone from there that?"

"I expect they would disagree."

As far as expectations went, the two men had theirs pleasantly dashed when they saw the camp itself. Neither men had properly slept under a roof for months and here were neatly spaced rows of huts of piping and corrugated iron lining groomed gravel paths. It really wasn't much to look at, a twenty-four foot tin can cut in half and laid on its side. The ends were capped with a pre-cut piece able to accommodate a door and two windows. One side, let in to from the path, was student billets- ending at a tarp drawn across the far quarter where Instructor-NCO's had their privacy, along with their own set of door and windows. Coming in from the student's end revealed a raised tongue and groove wood floor, bunks for twelve men and a stove which rested on a deep concrete plinth. A scarcity of coal meant they couldn't keep it alight at all times. This bothered them little as the inside was dry and draftless. Despite its lack of material or aesthetic, it rated far above any place they had been recently.

Felix and Ellins hadn't been the first to arrive, some lads from "C" Company had preceded them and had bagged the bunks by the windows. Fair enough, first in, was the thought, and the Buckshee men chose up next over, not too near the stove. That first day, knowing nothing more than which hut to report to; names checked against a sheet held by a purse-faced red cap at the gate post, they collected in this shed in order of arrival from whichever points of origin they'd been tossed. Some of them, God help them, were privates fresh from replacement depots. Tagged as men of potential, here they were to learn to lead without ever having heard an angry shot. Moose Jaw Camp was well outside the range of all but the biggest German guns, and those had more pressing targets. That being the case, it was well behind their own heavies, so even hearing outgoing shots was rare. Aside from a few weeks sleeping on the ground in bell tents around Etaples, these cubs had only just had a kip like this in the training camps in Kent. It showed in the way they creased the sheets and plumped the pillows. Felix unwound his crusted puttees, kicked off his clotted boots and peeled away ancient socks. Rough skin of calloused soles met smooth, newly varnished wood. Dry, God dammit, it was dry. Sitting at the end of his bed, both feet bare and firmly grounded, he actually felt a greet welling. How long had it been?

A drizzly, low hung and heavy summer's evening last year, when they'd all tumbled off a choppy and heaving passage and been herded into cavernous, empty warehouses by the harbour's rail yard. The gentle rain brought in from a seaward wind yielded in little plinks against the lead-lined panes of transoms, set high in the hope of keeping densely stacked commodities air chilled while awaiting their shipment. The only commodity stored there by that point was men, alighting from the familiar on a journey which was to divorce them entirely from what they had known about everything. This was a shift which had already begun long before this waypoint, merely in the purpose for which they had come. Over months at home and migrating an ocean, each step bringing them closer to what would shape their reality forever, something about everything to that point, that night in a dockside warehouse, just hadn't seemed as significant as hoped. Long before that first rip of fire from Spoon Farm; counting back to that seaside summer's night was where it had stopped feeling like a play, or a game, and a slowly germinating seed of who they were all to become within this epic took place over thought of adventure and frivolity. The very next morning, rail cars waiting to move them all south, their night in the warehouse became just one more leg of that journey towards an inescapable unknown.

From that to this, half a year later, not once had Felix had it so good. Trenches, bunkers and billets in the woods held no candle to the ecstasy of bare feet on bare wood.

"Aw, Bert, it's braw, inn't?"

"Nicer than I expected," Ellins admitted, but both had held further comment as it was then that the cubs had come in. So obviously out of place, one of the "C" Company boys asked if they were in the right hut. Shockingly clean, these fellows were a long look back down a dim hallway to what men they once had been, themselves a frightening glimpse of a future at life's end for those observing from untainted eyes. Felix coughed, and that really startled them. He hadn't been on cigarettes long enough to have acquired a smoker's hack. It was something else; a growling, phlegmy surge brought on from a long time breathing too close the air of other men- the dead as well as the living. Exposed to gas, the effluence of poisoned ground water and the steel reek of explosive air in terrible damp and razor's edge cold, such a cough was just one part of the body getting rid of the front line; a process not often completed before it was time to accumulate another layer on body, mind and soul. In essence, anyone who had spent as much time going through front line rotations as Felix, Bert Ellins and the four "C" Company cats carried bits of the front everywhere they went. Not only had they their Divisional and Brigade patches up on their shoulder, the elements had faded their colour. These tyros had been bounced around so much in an effort to get them to where they were needed hadn't landed anywhere long enough to know what colour it should be. Their buttons and brass titles shone. This was a result from a type of place known as "The Bull Ring." With reinforcements now coming in catch as catch can- both fresh from overseas and wounded or ill returning to duty, quick learning schools had been set up to orient the men to the front. By wide opinion they were reprehensible places of the most stunning attention to pettiness and ignorance of practicality that could be imagined. Felix had narrowly avoided a tenure in such a place only months ago, after he hoofed it from the hospital to find his unit rather than be put through such a pointless grist mill. Shined brass shows attention to detail and pride in deportment, both great qualities for a soldier, but shiny things had a knack for attracting unwanted attention from the visiting side, so his buttons and badges had been allowed to go

unpolished to just shy of tarnished. Tears and rips-
most of them benign as there were quite a lot of
sharp and jagged edges out there- had been sewn
according to each man's skill. Bert had more of a
sure hand at such things as Felix, and that leant a
garish quality to his dress. Not least of note was the
repaired seam on the left shoulder of his jacket. A
crenelated splinter from a trench mortar had split
that and roosted in his flesh, a wee Christmas
minding from Fritz that had him up in hospital for
Hogmanay. The officially sanctioned reminder of
that event was the thin dull gold braid above the cuff
of the same arm. Deeply matted stains of all manner
of source hung about almost as much fibre as that
which still could be kept clean. These, that resisted
laundering told their own tale of time and place, and
could be examined as a geologist determines the
fault line between ages. Dusty and blanched chalk
from the Somme formed the composite layer, dulling
but blending well with the dye of the serge. Then
there was deeply maroon speckles of blood; Sergeant
Merrick's, that German fellow Fern had stuck and
his own along that torn left shoulder. Overlaying
that was the fresher remains of the cloying, globbed
muck of land different than the Somme, a rich
topsoil above a thinner chalk strata, the lowlands

further north seeping drainage of the sea and dykes the Belgians had destroyed to preserve what little of their homeland they still clung to. Now with spring coming on this would only get worse. Throughout there were flecks of discolouration, the thread itself having lost its pigment in place of tiny yellow pink spots, which were actually the cleanest stains, his entire body having been bleached on occasion with chlorine. Felix also never went anywhere these days without his travelling circus. Nestled in any seam- no matter how poorly sewn- were legions of thirsty fleas. His nickname didn't have anything to do with the constant urge to soothe the itch left by little nips, everyone suffered from that equally, or in the case of the new lads, would soon enough.

In any event, the uncertainty of what was to follow, at least in the next few minutes was resolved by the first appearance of an instructor. Sergeant Keele put his head beyond the segregating tarp and pointed at one of the newest.

"You, there. Name?"

"Wilson, Sir."

"Sergeant," Keele corrected.

"Sorry."

"Shut up, Wilson. You are now Course Senior. Next timing is sixteen hundred. Have the Course formed up and ready to march to the Mess."

"How do I-" Wilson began, but Keele had vanished. So short was his presence that not one of them noticed until the next day that Sergeant Keele was missing his left arm from the elbow. His counterpart, Corporal Dufferin, was blind in one eye. Even though their attitude may have seemed a bit standoffish- much more so than any man, old or new had seen in training- it was a practised restraint, a granting of benefit of doubt. Those that were given a little latitude were watched to see if they used it to help themselves or took others into account first. So contrived was this method was that Sergeant Keele's arbitrary appointment of Wilson to get the men to dinner was a test of, in no particular order, Wilson's ability to solve the problem, the other student's willingness to help him succeed and on the man's ability to accept the help when needed. Throughout this two week evolution the thread that bound everything together- which was a conclusion that the men could only be coached so far to grasp, the balance of understanding having to be intrinsic- was that to lead was more than telling others what to do, it was a concept of making it seem what was being asked of others was the absolute right thing to do even when, perhaps especially when, not being convinced of the notion oneself. It lay, when properly done, somewhere between being a conjuror and a confidence man. Of the twelve bunks in their hut, three were empty by the morning of the parade where Felix had gotten his medal.

A fortnight followed of every moment so carefully arranged that those who Keele and Dufferin had turfed as not showing that potential were long forgotten in place of the practicalities even the most base level of the corporation required. Nothing, bar nothing in method was put to chance by the army, but they had a great way of hiding it. This was the problem with the army, as far as Felix was concerned; that the way in which it got things done was largely convoluted and not a little beyond what seemed to him as common sense. Sometimes, the modus operendi was as extraneous as being asked to solve long division problems using Roman numerals. Not impossible, but certainly not the simplest way of going about it. As everybody had already agreed to this arrangement at some point long before Felix took the shilling, he'd resigned himself to the mysteries of the machine. That was the rub, to go along with this, confounded, until perhaps the realisation that nothing was done in the army which wasn't deliberate set in; if it ever did. For Felix, this revelation meant that he knew everything had a purpose behind it even if that purpose often escaped him. What might seem needlessly confusing to initiates could prove perfectly logical and sound if properly explained, but the army was not a culture of making such explanations-again, deliberately-because initially all that was required of a soldier was discipline and obedience. They hadn't needed to know "why", so those elements which would provide that were left out as a matter of economy.

This course was entirely different, but at first it seemed much like any other day in the army. Each morning began with drill, but with the students taking turns in calling the marches, this being accompanied by lessons on the importance of drill; the building of a team and the need of that team to follow through on an abrupt decision heedless of confusion and fear. Days moved on into matters of ever increasing practicality- the qualities of leadership, the attack and the defense, their duties in billets and working parties. They learned about signals, writing reports and memoranda, the proper use of telephones (which required mastery of a bizarre shorthand of spoken English), and were introduced to the mechanics of map and compass. Much of what was being learned was not only new to the students, but the notion of giving such thorough preparation to junior leaders was just as new; part of a wholesale shift in tactical philosophy. For the first time, and in a very limited way, they were being asked to think.

The sheer speed and intensity of this carnal factory meant that any rigid adherence to old ideas could not be long tolerated. It had been a difficult lesson as it had cost so much blood to learn. It had begun, most locally for men of their experience with the Rifle Company ceasing to be the basic tactical unit for the infantry. When the war began, a Company Commander and his staff of officers had one hundred and twenty riflemen, or so, with an appropriate amount of NCO's to keep the rabble in line to work with. One hundred and twenty rifles, or so, made very little impact on prepared defenses and machine guns. Another issue was that placing the tactical base line at the Company level meant that the loss of command could throw the other ten dozen out of step. Losing two or three officers in a company in an action was likely not to end well for the rest of the rank and file. Withholding too strictly what an individual soldier needed to know or be capable of had long since stopped being economical. Shifting the baseline down a notch meant there could be four quasi-independent groups linked to a central command. The first benefit of giving Platoon Commanders tactical autonomy (within a certain limit) was that everybody could spread out more, take up a little more room, or, most hopefully, creating space that would make hitting all of them at once a little more difficult. Allied planners were compelled by what they faced in the prospect to break German lines to develop strategy to compete. The German notion was to halt the momentum of a large advance with overwhelming firepower, breaking up the attacking troops and weakening cohesion. If attacks devolved into a collection of isolated skirmishes, attention had to be given to tactical awareness and leadership at the lowest levels of organisation.

Going forward, working further out of direct command than had called for previously meant that each person in the platoon had to be prepared to step into another role in an instant. This stopped Felix worrying about the dread possibility of finding himself without Thorncliffe or Douglas and Six Platoon falling into his care and protection. He was still pretty sure he'd fuck it up, but was convinced he'd at least have a go at fucking it up as best he could. Felix was beginning to know both the how and the why of what was going to be required of him. All that remained was a practical examination.

Chapter XV

Constant rain pushed about by a cool north wind had only held off for the better part of the previous afternoon and this morning. The only clouds were being bustled, thin and whispy on that same cold air. A deep stand of trees lined the road, naked branches showing scant promise of renewal, but clicks whines and whistles of active wood pigeons, jackdaws and treecreepers gave hope of spring. Through the bare boughs, fans of light with little heat and chilly but slim shadows fell upon the road and the handful of idle soldiers standing to one side of the old stone laneway. Where the path to Moose Jaw Camp came to a "T" with the main thoroughfare which ran in almost a straight line to the front were the men Strachan and Ellins had been told to expect. Both of them had their course certificates in their haversacks, not twenty minutes prior had they been given them, in an abridged graduation ceremony at which they had also been given their first task as sanctioned leaders. Quite simply, they were to march a group of reinforcements to their battalion lines. Too new to be left of their own for a moment, these two dozen raw youths had come this far forward under the watchful eye of a sergeant from Brigade HQ.

"You lads Lance Corporals Ellins and Strachan, 'B' Company, 279th?" He'd asked, ignorantly giving full value to all the consonants in the latter's name. Strachan had this happen so frequently, he all but ignored it when dealing with people he'd not likely see again. Far too many times, particularly at the beginning of his training, he'd have to answer the roll with "Sir," to indicate his presence, and then "it's 'Straw'n', Sir." Right from that genesis, the other fellows began intentionally mis-speaking his name to get a rise from him. Along the way, it was thought to be amusing to transpose the sounds to come up with "Scratchin'." It may even have been Ferguson who'd started that. As an effort to circumvent the teasing, he'd encouraged his new friends to call him by his first name.

"Which is?" One had asked.

"Felix."

"What? That's a name you'd give a cat." Thus, he acquired his nom-de-guerre.

The sergeant from headquarters' name was Smith, and had little sympathy for those with difficult handles. In any case, it was Ellins who answered in the affirmative.

"Good," the sergeant said, and pointed at the men he'd brought here, "these belong to you, now." Handing over a clipboard grasping sheaves of loose-leaf he added, "They're listed here, name and number. Give this list to your adjutant, and let him know their files will be sent with the next battalion dispatch."

Ellins nodded, took the sheets from him, and now that his duties had been discharged, the sergeant took upon a look of someone who wanted to be elsewhere and had nothing stopping him from doing so. He left, moving swiftly in the direction opposite the other's intended route without further comment. Felix sidled up to Bert, who was flipping through the paperwork.

"Would you look at them, Bert?" They were remarkable. Much like those fellows from course, these men here were direct from the Bull Ring, but unlike those recent classmates, hadn't been selected for any outstandingness other than availability. True, one or two among them were returning wounded- Felix saw one of them had three wound stripes up, but none had been with the King's Own before. The remainder could claim each step from here as the closest they'd ever been to the front, and they were still miles back. Freshly painted helmets rested at unsure angles atop heads home to slightly bewildered eyes. The irony of uniformity, as in the attempt to get everyone to look alike, meant that their new battle dress was equally ill-fitting in one ratio to another, man to man. Accentuating this, and what Felix had drawn Bert to was, aside from the old sweats among them, each had been issued the 1914 Pattern Infantry Equipment. At the start of the war, the British textiles industry was not able to meet the demand for equipping such a rapidly growing army. What could was the leather workers, and a replica of the standard cotton-twill web harness fashioned with treated hide was authorised. Put under government contracts, saddlers and cobblers throughout Britain were soon able to make up for any deficiencies in quantity. Despite functioning in the same way, the difference in material made the new kit dreadfully unsuitable. The front was ravenous for leather, all the damp, rot and mud wore away at cowhide like acid. Even if it were possible to avoid getting it ruined in that way, the straps were tighter, more inflexible and hard to fit properly, particularly when wet. Worse even was the leather cartridge pouches held less ammunition than the '08 Pattern like Felix's. The official line on this kit was that it wasn't intended for field use, but here they were, in the field, being used.

"We'll have to see about getting them properly kitted out." Ellins agreed, thinking they'd also have to get them in kilts. No sense in sending them on any scheme until they all blended in. German snipers were particularly drawn to such contrasts. At least their rifles weren't as new. Each had a patina and wear on the stock, a little knocked about, but these weapons had all proved more resilient than their previous operators. Those that wielded them now had perhaps fired only fifty live rounds in training.

"Well," said Ellins, "best get moving. You're senior, you want to take it?" The other shrugged, an attempt at nonchalance rather than indecisiveness.

"I suppose. Stand by me, then." Ellins obligingly placed himself beyond Felix's elbow, whose gaze now scanned the scattering before him. "Alright, you lot, on your feet. Sling arms everywhere." He inserted a pause, which allowed him to catch a few faults. "Up here we sling muzzle down, keep the dirt off." Only half of them had breech covers, protective canvas sheaths over the bolt, in place. Felix halted and inwardly berated himself for overlooking detail. "If you have them, put your breech covers on." While they went about this, those that had to, Felix eye settled on the tallest one in the gaggle.

"You! You're my Right Marker. Fall in opposite me." When he was in place, Felix hollered for the rest of them to form fours, which they did without little fuss, scurrying about to space themselves properly. Once settled, Felix centred himself and drew a deep breath, about to give his first proper instructions.

"Good morning. I am Lance Corporal Strachan, and this is Lance Corporal Ellins. You men are now with 'B' Company, the King's Own Canadian Scots. We will be taking you down this road towards our Battalion rest area. A few things before we go. We can do this at the easy step so long as you all sharpen up if we see an officer. Where we're headed is about a mile and a half from the front line; we are considerably further back where we are now. These roads are all known to Fritz and they do get bombed frequently. You new lads clock on to me, Ellins or any of the ol' fellahs with ya. If we go to ground, follow suit." He noticed some of them looking at the earth beneath them. The road itself was of dark stones, subject to decades of weather and traffic these had been worn down to a glassy sheen. Seasonal changes over the better part of the last hundred years shifted the even distribution of cobbles so that the whole length had no true surface, but dips and rises which interrupted the engineered camber and allowed snow, rain and melt water to collect in the recesses. Every now and again, the odd corner of a stone stood up dangerously waiting to catch a misplaced foot or hoof, or jostle iron wheels. Damp and shade inspired moss to creep through the space between stones, a forest in miniature. Either side was swamped with swollen drainage. The thaw and the rains had carried with them deep mud and any other rubbish swept along its oozing path. Low ground here made the passage of run off difficult, and the overflow stood stagnant and ripe for several feet beyond the road. Some of the men had looks of contempt at what they might be expected to drop into on short notice.

"I wouldn't worry about that mess. Time comes, you won't think twice. Same for respirators. If we put 'em on, so do you- and damn well make sure your mates know as well. Do not remove them until you are properly instructed. Once we set off, no smoking; and if any wan of ye breaks out singing, I'll thrash ye." He turned to Ellins and lowered his voice. "How's that?"

"Nice touch about the singing."

"Can't stand that shite. Rank hath its privileges."

"Shall we?"

"Oh, but of course." He turned back to his parade. "Troops! At ease to your right. By the left, easy march," he ordered, eleven words being sufficient to face them all in the proper direction and send them forward at a sauntering pace.

For a good long while, there was little to listen to save the grinding of tacked boots on stone. A gentle voice picked up, a man in the rank closest to Felix, somewhat behind.

"Have a word, Lance Corporal?" Felix paused to put himself in lock step with him, the man with three ribbons on his cuff.

"What is it?"

"We're straight down from Etaples, haven't stopped since leaving the Ring. That's near fifty miles by train, wagon and foot by now. These kids are alright, if not a bit fagged out. There was no issue of hard rations or ammunition before we set off, we've not got a bullet between us; and you've seen that Fourteen Pattern *dechetes*."

"Can't do anything to rest the men until we get there, same with ammo. I don't think it'll be a problem to get that at Battalion. The kit we'll do what we can to replace." Ammunition and rations were doled out with few qualms. Other items, ones perhaps the soldier may not be strictly entitled to tended to be more difficult to acquire. Usually this wasn't for a lack of the desired item, but more frequently from the quartermaster's assumed ownership over the stores. Their level of responsibility meant serious consequences if inventory was mishandled, so tight-fisted men were ideal, but all too often such frugality had a way of making it seem that giving out kit personally impoverished them. A distinct possibility was that their Regimental Quartermaster Sergeant-Major, Richardson might not actually have two dozen sets of webbing going spare, even if he could be convinced to give them out.

"You ask me, Corp, sending out this many all at once can only mean one thing."

"I see what you mean."

"Not only that, they were practically scraping the Ring clean. Hundreds have been passed out over the last week. I don't doubt we'll get what we need, but I think we're going to need it sooner than we can get it." Felix, away as he was on course had heard nothing about large movements of reinforcements. There was no betting against the balloon going up very soon indeed. Good information to have, and could be some leverage in prising essential stores from Richardson's grip.

"Ta," he said, "Handy to know that."

"San fairy ann."

"What's your name, Troop?"

"Tremaine, Corp." Felix made a mental note, and stepped out to put himself back to the lead. Tremaine's observance was on point- there could be no question that the attack they'd been working towards was now irrevocably imminent. This, of course, had never been in doubt. Months of patrols, raids and rehearsals told their own tale of what was to come, always growing in intensity and urgency as time moved forward. Now, this notion was not something which was yet to happen, it now was something about to happen. Each outgoing artillery shot could be the herald for the preparatory bombardment. Twenty-four men for one company all at once was remarkable on its own, but it wasn't just these reinforcements, nor was it the hundreds Tremaine had seen put on the march.

Thousands, tens, hundreds of thousands were on the move, along the entire length of the line. All the nations at war, their Dominions and Colonies, vast numbers of men, some of whom now concentrated in France were representative of the highest population of their nationalities outside of only their largest home cities, were moving towards a superlative and as the French General, now in command of all these millions of men, Nivelle, had promised, a war winning battle. Felix didn't put his thoughts on that grand of a scale, but just knowing that something very big and very important was close to hand was fodder enough for his mind. Despite his months at the front, he had only ever been in one real fight-Spoon Farm. Admittedly, much had happened since then, but nothing like on the scale of that past event and certainly not anywhere near what was coming. While he had some reasonable expectations based upon his experience, everything new, in method, his rise in responsibility- still remained an unknown quality. That being so, the combination of a number of things leading to his personal uncertainty sat with him so much he couldn't be sure if he envied these new men their hopeful ignorance or not.

Soon, they had left the woods behind them and came into the open, untilled fields stretching out on either side of the road. Some distance ahead, a motor lorry was parked just beyond the verge. Felix had seen it straight off, knew what it was and cringed. In a moment they would pass it and all of them would know, and then the chatter would start. Once the lettering on the side was seen, or the whiff of tea was perceived, the marching stomachs would begin to grumble. Felix was examining the sky, even though he knew it was useless to predict a shelling as one would oncoming rain. Unbidden, from a swallowed memory, he found he had tensed, the edges of his sling pinching deep into a palm moving into a fist. The murmur had gone from front to rear as each file saw what they would shortly be abreast of. At long last, someone was brave enough to address the situation.

From the back came "Time for the tea wagon, Lance Corporal?" Felix didn't really hear that plea, distracted by something else, from inside the vault of things he tried not to think about. That face, distorted in fear beyond abject terror- animalistic- stuck, and screaming:

"For the love of God, somebody help me!" Then nothing, blankness. In the present, his pace picked up sharply, a scowl drew up on his lips.

"No. There'll be no tea wagon." The words snapped out harder than was his habit. "And no talking in ranks!" Which put an end to the issue and the YMCA volunteers were bypassed with no further comment. In silence, they continued to crunch along the road.

Chapter XVI

Captain Lafferty felt he was fighting a losing battle. His office, the Battalion Orderly Room, defied its title. A windowless room let into by a thick wood door, a small hole had been knocked through the corridor wall from which a tangle of telephone wires spilled out and traced their way to the company posts in town and action stations much further forward. His signallers were constantly in motion, following the trace of wires to find breaks- which would cut out the current- or going along with spade in hand to bury them in the hope of protecting fragile copper wire from the elements; which included German shells. Usually, half of his signals section would be at this, the other taking calls as they came in. These days, there were nearly daily requests from higher to send out linesmen to help install the untold miles of telephone networks for the expected offensive, such that Captain Lafferty was stuck trying to manage the calls himself much of the time. Stacks of folders, piled upon any available surface were spilling over each other and mingled among reports, requisitions and returns. All were wanting proper filing and the sooner he could put everything where it belonged, the sooner he could update the Battalion War Diary, which Colonel Sinclair needed to sign off on a daily basis. That Lafferty had just come back from a short leave in Paris would make no difference. His clerks had done the best they could in his absence, but much of his job was outside their ken, required an officer's input or could only be properly done by the Adjutant personally. Lieutenant Weybridge, the intelligence officer, and Lafferty's immediate junior had tried his best in his absence, but as he wasn't really a bright spark, anything he didn't know how to accomplish had been left undone in anticipation of his boss's return. More men on the job would have helped, except that the mere closet Lafferty had been given was not conducive to large gatherings. In yet another case of having to make do, the Adjutant was stuck with the room. Relocating wasn't possible, he had to be proximate to the Colonel's office, across the hall. A substantially grander affair, the beautifully appointed parlour the mare had used for receiving visitors now played permanent host to Sinclair out of the line. As the Hotel still functioned as a municipal building as well as a Battalion Headquarters, there wasn't anywhere within its walls that would suit him better which wasn't already used. If all the aspects of his job could be put on a low boil for a few minutes, he might be a little further ahead. No sooner would he reduce one pile to have a new one begin, or any one or, more likely several, telephones would ring, distant, tinny voices demanding more of him; or someone would present themselves to him with yet further matters trying his time.

"You see it's a bit of a state here," he said, not by way of apology, his hands full of paperwork, "so I'm just going to run you through verbally. Do you have your course certificate?"

Strachan reached into his haversack and presented the document. The Adjutant took it, and searched for a spot to put it for the time being. One pile was just as good as another, he decided, and left it with the topmost layer on his desk.

"Good work," he continued, opening a drawer and taking out a set of chevrons. "Colonel Sinclair has authorised me to inform you that you've been promoted to corporal. Congratulations." Lafferty's tone was perfunctory. Strachan took his stripes.

"Thank you, Sir. I'll put them up straight away."

"See that you do. Those new men still outside?'

"Yes, Sir." Strachan had parked them out front of the Hotel du Ville and had gone in to hand the nominal list the HQ sergeant had given out, expecting to be on his way back to Sheepy Baa Woods, but it appeared that Captain Lafferty had more to tell him.

"Right- take eight of them and report to Mister Thorncliffe," he paused, still only halfway attending to the new corporal and the wreck of his office. "That's it, Corporal. Send in Ellins. I'll get your certificate back to you as soon as I get it logged in your file." Strachan hesitated. It was plain that Captain Lafferty was behind on all fronts, but the younger man didn't know when next he'd have a chance to be face to face with the Adjutant, the very man who could help his cause. Lafferty looked up.

"You still here? Disappear, Corporal."

"I'd like to put in a request." Captain Lafferty looked incredulous.

"What, now? Can it wait?"

"Small thing, Sir. I'd like to ask that my brother be transferred to this Regiment when he comes overseas."

"I see. And where is he now?"

"That new training camp, Sir- North of Toronto, I think."

"You mean he hasn't left Canada yet?"

"No, Sir."

"Corporal Strachan, you're a thin edge away from wasting my time. If your brother was at a depot in England, I may have been able to see my way about it. Even then, at this extent, I can tell you the Colonel himself is pleased with what we're sent whenever we can get it. He hasn't a spare moment to give me to pluck one man from a bunch."

"Yes, Sir. I apologise for interrupting you with this. I'd like to say, though, that I would be in your debt. My mother would be in your debt." It was as close to begging as dignity allowed. He turned to leave.

"Just a moment, Corporal." Lafferty took a folded sheet from his breast pocket, its contents the reason why Colonel Sinclair had given the Captain time off, and let it fall to his desk. "I understand you. That, Corporal, is a letter from my Aunt telling me my brother, Hugh, was killed during actions in December. My aunt wrote because my father has collapsed with melancholy. The army will send your brother where it will. If I can help, I shall; but let me put this to you: Do you really think having him with you will ensure his safety? You've seen it yourself to know that death out here is arbitrary. Luck, skill, intellect, even love can't change that." He sniffed, trying to hide his own despair, but Strachan saw it. There was nothing less to him for it, as they both felt very much the same way; the way of very tired men who still had uncountable misery before them.

Having taken up more of the Adjutant's attention than he properly should have, Strachan braced up, saluted and let himself out into the corridor. Such was the way of having to leave the room backwards, he collided with Major McCowan, who, in all honesty, hadn't been paying attention to where he was going either.

"Oh!" He exclaimed as they bumped. "Terribly sorry." Then he saw who it was. "Ah, hello, Felix," quickly correcting himself when he noticed the new chevrons the man had clutched in his hand, "or is it Corporal Strachan?"

The other demurred. "I prefer 'Felix' from you, Padre."

"So do I." The slender parson leaned towards him and winked. "I'm only in this suit as it seems to be the prevailing fashion." While this generated a smile on Felix, McCowan changed to a bit of a graver tone. "I did need to see you, Felix. Rather afraid I'm having to give you a difficult job. You remember when we last spoke, about your brother James?"

Felix nodded. "Coincidence can be a terrible thing. I've just had word that one of your men has lost his brother. From what I understand their mother is unwell. The army has decided to grant him a hardship discharge." He passed a telegram to Felix.

He read it. It was a notice from the Red Cross in Switzerland, explaining that the man in question had passed of pneumonia in a prison camp somewhere in Germany.

"If you don't feel up to bearing this news, I understand. Either way, please send Philip to see me straight away." This news did little to settle Felix's mind. Within five minutes he'd been told of two men losing their brothers. At the very least, though, Squeak would be going home. It was, of course, a terrible reason; but home was home. Anything away from this mess was a considerable improvement.

He stepped out from the dusty entrance hall of the Hotel de Ville, itself an old heap of dusty brick, accented in plaster coated stone. It had never been directly hit, but constant concussion of close bursts – and in no small order, the nearby heavies- had peeled away great chunks of the cornice, ground to the grey particulate which hung about the place. It was the seat of power, locally and was, except for the rectory of Sainte Gertrude, the most imposing feature of Petit Rejour; slightly more tumbledown than it once was. Tar shingles had shed in patches, the clock on the edifice was stopped, first at the hour and minute the town had heard they were at war, and more permanently when its gears and springs had been given up for the effort, as had its jolly iron bell. Blinking in the bright sun Felix approached the reinforcements he had left in the forecourt. He counted out his eight, telling them to follow him and leaving the rest in place while Bert Ellins had his turn with the Adjutant. Down Petit Rejour's main street they went, to the edge of town where the path became "Avenue Road" and ran into Sheepy Baa Woods. After two weeks away, it felt so wonderfully familiar to be in this place, despite its damp and reek, the sprawl of men living rough. As he brought the men into the platoon camp, he beamed brightly at the first familiar face he saw.

"Hey, Kelley! How's things?" O'Leary was impassive as usual. "Mind watching these fellahs for a minute? I should report to Thorncliffe."

"Okay."

"Oh, have you seen Squeak? The Padre wants to speak to him." The older man's stony face betrayed an unusual modicum of emotion.

"Missing."

"What?"

"Went out on a bombing party yesterday. Him and Fern with some guys from Nine Platoon. Nobody's come back yet."

"Fern? When did he return?"

"Week after you started course."

"And he took Squeak on a raid?" Again, O'Leary nodded, but seemed a bit confused.

"What's wrong with that?"

"More than I'd care to think about." Felix would have to leave that hanging right now, but with an uneasiness brought on by the secret he carried. Immediately he found Lieutenant Thorncliffe, dozing in his beach chair.

"Sir?" Strachan prodded, the officer stirred.

"Hmm? Ah, Catscratch, it's you."

"Yes, Sir. Just back from course. Ellins will be along shortly. I brung you a present."

"What? Really?" Strachan nodded, pointed to the eight new men and Thorncliffe couldn't hide his pleasure. "God damn, that's a sight. Can only be bad news coming when I get my Platoon topped up all at once, but, still," he stopped mid-thought. "Did you already hear about Ferguson and Pippin?"

"O'Leary just told me, Sir."

"Let's keep our fingers crossed. The bombing party has only been missing a few hours, they may turn up yet." Strachan agreed.

"I certainly hope so."

"Until then, we're still short. I was going to shuffle some men between sections, you know, to spread out the experience. Will you be okay with just taking one of those reinforcements?" A daft question, Strachan thought, because how he felt really had no effect on the situation. Presently, he made a non-committed noise, then said,

"I'll take Tremaine, Sir."

"Suits me."

"I'm concerned about their equipment, Sir." Thorncliffe rarely missed a trick and had already noticed the most obvious deficiency.

"Noted. Don't worry about that, Sergeant Douglas will be on top of it shortly. I'll have him send you a needle and thread, Corporal." In a gesture of congratulation he offered his hand, a courtesy rarely extended between the army's two castes. Strachan parted with him and took Tremaine to his Section's area.

"You seem a decent sort," Tremaine had said on the way, "so I'm a bit out as to why we passed on the tea wagon, right after we talked about the lads having had nothing to eat. I mean, I'm sure you didn't do it out of cruelty."

"No, of course not. You've been around, I'll bet you've got the odd thing what sets a twitch. Mine's tea wagons. Don't like hanging around them- don't like stopping anywhere along a road on the march."

"One of those things, yes, I get it."

"You know where 'Whip Crack Crossing' is?" This was a notorious locale, a busy intersection that was frequently targeted by harassing German fire; a safe wager that a few random shells would cause a great deal of havoc. Such was its reputation that drivers had taken to getting past the radial as quickly as they, or their teams, could be persuaded to move. Tremaine was no stranger to it.

"That's where I got my second 'blighty'."

"Hmm. Well, once saw a 'Y' wagon get blown to shite there."

"Once bitten, eh?" Felix agreed, wanting to move past the subject lest that image would materialise. Tremaine read the path of conversation well. "Okay, thanks, Corp. I won't bring it up again. But since you've been straight with me, I'll let you know that you may have hand-picked me for your section on an assumption."

"What do you mean?"

"You see these wound stripes and think, 'here's a fellow what's seen his bit.' Sure, I've been sent up to hospital three times, but I'm not a front-hog like you. I'm a farrier."

"Oh, grief. You've never been forward?"

"Not any further than the gun line, and each time I've been hit." He tried to make light of this. "It would appear I don't even know enough to duck. This is going on a lot. The army's long on cooks, clerks and smiths but short on guys like you. I think it's called 'a balance of resources.'" Promises from the top about filling the troop order before the start of spring offensives had to be delivered somehow. For these powers that be, one battalion brought up to full strength was but a drop in the bucket of a host of multitudes with a treacherous hole in the bottom. Troops were being sent to the front as soon as they could be declared 'trained'. These numbers were deficient, to say nothing about their declared status sometimes being not much more than a minimum standard of the term. Remaining spots could be taken by wounded who were just fit enough for duty and, as in Tremaine's case, by canvassing service and support units for possible converts to riflemen.

"Yeah, but nobody would assume I could shoe a horse if it were the other way 'round. Alright, Tremaine, stick by me for the time being and don't be feart to ask questions. Don't think yerself daft for doing so. Better to feel a bit silly than going a cropper for pride's sake."

"My mates call me 'Tremor.'" An eyebrow raised. "Nothing to it, I got steady hands, wouldn't work out for me otherwise, professionally. Just a play on my name."

"Oh, I get that. When no one important is looking, I answer to 'Catscratch.'"

A soldier's time is only very rarely their own, and as much as Felix could grow exasperated by the constancy of having one thing to do after the next, his by no means was a solitary condition. Something had once been said about idle hands, and the army took that notion wholeheartedly in what may look as either a maximization of resources, a willingness to treat humans as chattel, or somewhere in between depending on how far that system had worn down resistance to cynicism. Felix held forth with the best of them as to how they were driven, day and night, and could use a few minutes to gather breath. In actuality, having nothing to do of any consequence, particularly if it was a task that could be done without dedicating a large mental effort, as desirable as that was, could sometimes be worse. When the mind wandered, it often went places Felix preferred it wouldn't.

It turned out that the Lieutenant wasn't kidding about the sewing, and shortly after dinner Felix could be found, sitting against a tree, perforating his fingers, accidentally passing the needle several times through both sides of the sleeve, sewing it shut. Seeing the YMCA lorry this morning, and then that chat with Tremaine, perhaps he should have expected his memory to land square on that awful, inerasable tableau. Like today, it had been bright, fairly clear, the sky a marbled blue dome punctuated by the sun's providence of mid-winter light; brief and weak, but bright enough to dazzle frozen puddles and the sweeping patches of dirty snow. At the hospital, the doctor had been a bit surprised. Felix's shoulder had been pinked, but the splinter wasn't in too deep. A good, hard yank with forceps threw it loose, almost as a dentist would pull a rotten tooth.

"Don't see why your Regimental Surgeon couldn't have done that; save you coming all this way."

"He was otherwise busy, Sir." When last Felix had seen Doctor Salinger, the surgeon was wrist deep in the twitching mass of the man who had taken more than his share of the trench mortar; the wee splinter of little bother was Felix's portion. One of the stretcher bearers looked at it quickly, and shoved him in the direction of out of the bloody way. Thorncliffe came along and just told Felix to hop it on his own to the Casualty Clearing Station. A light priority, once there he'd been grouped with other 'petite blesse' until enough of them could be moved along to Base Hospitals.

For something that Salinger may have been able to do within minutes of the hit, his unavailability drew Felix's treatment out over several days. The bad news, with a great deal of perspective that he was still around to get any news at all, was Felix missed out on the Regimental Christmas Dinner. That affair had been held after the Holiday itself, as they'd been up front. Friendly international football matches were now so much as reaching mythical. Having happened, two years ago, time had gone to see the final exit of many who shook hands in the '14 truce as to push it into being almost beyond living memory. Precisely why there was iron flying about-both sides contributing in equal measure- was to not allow the enemy to be humanised, or sympathised. As it happened, the day hadn't gone completely without observance. It hadn't been half an hour before Felix had been hit that Ferguson had thrust an awkwardly shaped parcel at him.

"Happy Christmas, Felix."

Wrapped in brown paper, the gift was solid and heavy in Felix's hands.

"Go on, open it," his friend encouraged. The paper was only roughly folded around the object inside and was shed quite easily, to reveal a trench knife much like the one Ferguson had used to dispatch the German brute who had taken Felix off his guard in that raid a fortnight before.

"Wait, Andy, is this yours?"

"Yep. I want you to have it."

"That's very kind, but I've not anything to give you in return."

"Don't worry about it. Maybe with it in your hands, you might be around for next Christmas. You can make it up to me then. I could do with a nice watch."

"Oh, sure, if either of us lasts that long."

"You have a knack for taking the fun out of things, Felix, d'you know that?"

Felix might have rebutted that he was only being pragmatic, but he'd no notion such a word existed.

"I'm stepping out for a smoke," he said, tucking the knife into the waist band of his kilt. "Ta very much, Andy; very grand of you."

"San fairy ann," Ferguson replied; which was a recent addition to soldier's slang, corrupted from the French "Ca ne fait rein"- "It's nothing at all."

Oh, the Regimental Dinner would have been grand; the men invited into the great hall at the Hotel de Ville, served and stood drinks by the officers, the Colonel replaced by the youngest private for the day. It wasn't a cheerless season altogether for him. While still awaiting the go ahead to return to his unit, Felix was first footed by his cousin Billy. They had a good laugh, and got some pictures taken together to send home to the folks. Billy had wasted most of the day in trying to get a bottle and tracking Felix down to toast the New Year, he'd have to get back to his battery before he could stay too long. With half of whatever it was Billy had promised was some kind of whiskey peeling through the steel , no doubt, of Felix's water bottle, they shook hands, said nothing, parted ways.

It was a Hell of a slog from where they kept the hospitals to where Felix lived and worked. Hook and eye closures on the collar were the first thing to be loosened, once the hospital grounds were to his back. Problem with that was the helmet's strap could feel just as confining, but he'd long since come to live with that, his issue Brodie now sporting the blow where what could have been worse hadn't happened. The shoulder was bad enough, still quite stiff, it was too tender to take turns on his slung rifle and his right arm was cramping under the sustained weight over distance, Billy's gift did nothing but give him a dizzying thirst, so once he saw the tea wagon, still a ways off, Felix stepped out to close up a little faster. A queue was around the back end of the truck, whose hinged panel along the side was folded down, allowing several to be served at once. Whiskey flipped his stomach, and he stopped, at first in the way he sometimes could feel a hiccough coming and the misbelief he could do something to prevent it, he remained motionless once he realised where he had come to. Oh, didn't it serve him right for marching out half in the bag? This was Whip Crack Crossing, no mistake. Roads fed in and out, their confluence a circular track around where a signpost had once stood. The signs had been taken down during the French retreat to the Marne in the war's first days; the timber to which they'd been nailed was fractured to a small stub. This place was almost moon-like, with a pocked and gouged surface. Only the roads were attempted to be kept level, but no crew was at that as Felix came to it. How this Y truck had come to be this far forward could only be summed up to ignorance or grave misfortune. When he started forward, and those getting hot cups were more clearly in view it was apparent that these were the very men that should have been pointing the feckless away from danger. Tea and jam pieces, cigarettes, all were being hurriedly transacted, so it seemed that this section from Brigade Provost had met that obligation, but didn't have any qualms about getting what they could before they moved the truck off. They'd come down from the support line after going up to collect a prisoner. Some ne'er do well had done something silly, and, worse, had been caught. Now, he was paying for it, in that particular way of the army. Given a spell of Field Punishment Number One, the young fellow in the escort was required to fulfill his usual duties, as much extra work as could be shoehorned into the gaps, such as they were, and in between all of that, he could be-was in fact, required to be- restrained to a fixed object. Here, a fence post sufficed and the prisoner stood, looking a bit sheepish, off to one side; his hands bound and trussed like a bridle hitch. Back and forth along their direction of march, the officer among them paced in nervous bounds and obsessively consulted his watch.

Felix really didn't want to be where he was anymore, the rot-gut, fatigue and being among so many things waiting to go wrong all begged his leave. When it did go wrong, it began as if it were surreal. The whine of the first shell he felt rather than heard, the hair on his neck standing on edge, and he was in the ditch, doing his shoulder no favours, slightly before the burst. More bark than bite, it went off afield settling as a wave of heavy air shuddering through the surroundings. Felix stayed where he was, the Provost detachment quickly taking ground where the tea wagon was belatedly abandoning a station it had been in error of taking up in the first place. Let that truck get past, Felix had thought. Maybe that shell was a one off. It wasn't. He heard the fall this time, a long way off, taking its time and with a pushing crush threw itself on the road, thick dislodged cobbles raining down. Felix pressed himself into his saving ground, air stolen from his lungs, a sucker punch of vacuum. If he knew of a better hole, he was in no mood to go to it, his life resigned to mathematics. Size of gun, weight of charge, range, bearing, trajectory, temperature, relative humidity, elevation above sea level for both the point of shot and intended target and so many more variables were all up for grabs, and even if Felix had been given the values, he would need a week to do the arithmetic. He couldn't have counted his fingers right then, instinct compelling him to breath, his lungs not cooperating and a dark edge on his vision, he could now barely hear anything, but he heard the next whine. He now curled, to no purpose other than the childish feeling that by doing so he made himself smaller. Again he was at the bottom of a deep well, again ages passed with the scream, above the noise of the truck's engine struggling to find gear, ending both when they met. It became, all of it, beyond the blink of an eye, flinders scattered about the cross roads, no one piece retaining a semblance of what it had been. Felix's lungs were afire now, the pressure, and the smut, all giving him a very short outlook on all things relating to continued existence. Throughout, there was another persistent thing, a screaming, apart from the shells; a hollering, really, a desperate, continuous noise. Now, in that suspended instant between a then, full of possibilities and a now made up of only one possibility, the plea came as a dog might howl the words "For the love of God, somebody help me!" The prisoner, the poor wretched man, was regaining his feet after some jetsam of the tea wagon had struck his forehead, all but scalping him. The blood was piping forth horrendously, painting his strained face a deeper frothy pink, although he had no notion of that at all. Every ounce of effort and being was put towards trying to get the knots free, kicking the post attempting to knock it loose, and without let that singular appeal that no one would answer. Felix saw the fourth shot as it came in, while he was looking towards the stuck man, still screaming,

"For the love of God, somebody help me!" A jarring blast was followed by still more filthy airless heat, Felix swooned, but he couldn't hear the screaming anymore. Nothing moved for a good long while. Whole minutes passed of irregular silence. Slowly, men began to peek out, the world ever so gamely setting itself back to rights. Giving his head a shake, and finding nothing that rattled, Felix came up to his feet, though they felt a bit wobbly. A quick check assessed that he had all he had brought with him, that poor bastard at the fence nothing but a rag clotted smear; and his hands, reposed, still firmly affixed to the post. Felix's thoughts washed themselves from the shell's knockabout and became singularly clear- to put as much distance as he could between here and anywhere else, and, he intended to be right quick about it too. He could process this all later, or not, just as long as he'd have the option to do so.

"Hang on a moment," someone had said, and if Strachan hadn't seen it was that officer, he wouldn't have stopped. "Where are you off to?"

"Returning to unit from hospital, Sir."

"Um," he produced a notebook, a pocket sized compendium fair bulging with added pages, dog ears and cryptic bookmarks, "I'd like your name and outfit, Lance Corporal. There may be an inquiry."

"Nine seven two two three nine, Strachan, F, D. King's Own Canadian Scots."

"Thank you. Carry on, Lance Corporal."

Felix hurried to move off, glad that salutes were forbidden in the field, for his contempt outweighed propriety. Figuring he had put enough distance and still be heard, Felix stopped. "If I'm called to an inquiry, I'll tell 'em that there may be folk dead now what would be alive if your lot hadn't gone for tea." No note, Felix saw, was made of that, the officer seeming quite stunned by his frankness. "And I'll tell any Casualty Station I pass to send back stretcher bearers to look after this mess, as you seem stood there looking after yourself."

Lieutenant Osgoode could say nothing of that, his mind didn't seem to be working at the same speed as things were happening.

Slivering through the tough layer of skin at the side of his thumb with the needle, Felix held back before his hand became part of his jacket was well. It was getting on to dark by the time he was nearly done when somebody stood in what little light he had left. When Felix looked up to tell whoever it was to clear off, he saw, covered in dried blood, that it was Ferguson.

Chapter XVII

Weary, a long chain of events having defined his day, Ferguson folded his legs under him to sit next to Felix. He smacked parched lips.

"Got a smoke?"

"That's what you're opening with? Where the Hell is Pippin?"

"I didn't think he'd make it back."

"So that's not him all over you?" Ferguson shook his head 'no.'

"Staff Sergeant Belfry. The whole day's been a real bag drive. D'you have a smoke or not?" Felix brought out his pack.

"What happened out there?"

In the same bright morning that Felix had come from Moose Jaw Camp to Sheepy Baa Woods, one of a handful of bombing parties was a bit behind on its schedule. The map had noted their intended target and was straightforward enough, it was the German observation post that had been carefully concealed. Belfry had begun to believe it was his failure at orienteering, before he became convinced they had been in the right spot all along, but now it had become day break and these men were not within throwing distance. A steady drizzle over the past few days had softened the ground and moistened the air, a humidity of chilling damp hung about; the day wouldn't become warm enough to lift it skyward. In shallows, it grew thick enough to condense to mist. Otherwise it was too sparse to be anything than droplets clinging to wool, wood and steel. What could made its way back to the smudge of lightening sky, and though there hadn't been any today, Staff Sergeant Belfry and his party were as wet in this thick morning as they would be had it come to rain. Even the flies seemed lethargic, sticking closely in large colonies of boated insects, roosting on anything more still than they. Belfry had checked his watch, at the right minute he could move again. The delay in finding their target was an upset, but not critically so. It only made the move to the throwing point a bit trickier. For half an hour or so, he held his men in a little fold, waiting for the morning stand-to to come to an end. When the front relaxed into its daily routine, there would be enough to distract errant eyes and the last leap to the throwing point could be attempted. The wet had unlocked the mud, and each step forward was an unsettling squelch; for the chance of the sound giving them away or a queasiness at what gruesomeness their footsteps might uncover.

All the big raids had stopped. Nothing more could be gained from them; the Divisional sized affairs early in March had been a bit of a last hurrah. German defenses had been exquisitely surveyed, prisoners brought back had told all they knew. Risking men to this extent this close to the beginning of a major offensive would have been beyond all sense. Although, gaining intelligence, either in what was seen in enemy trenches during a raid, or from prisoners snatched could only go so far as to be truly beneficial and would not have been reason enough to continue the practice on static enemy formations. A very real purpose of carrying on with raids was the need to shake the funk out of men who were otherwise not moving about much. Show them that the enemy line could be pierced, that aggressiveness could outlast fear, their opponents were only flesh and blood, and if a few men met their ends, their mates would be easy to push towards vengeance. The coming attack as a whole was no surprise. It was futile to expect such massive preparations could go unnoticed. Perhaps the best that could be hoped for would be to keep the time and date of commencement a well-kept secret. To that end, completely ceasing the harassment of the enemy by means of raids could signal such an operational change. Taking the fight to targets of priority- such as this observation post- would continue to unsettle Fritz, keep him guessing and as a bonus, eliminating a spot that would be the first alerted by the advance, when it came. This was enough on its own to require it being dealt with, the decision being to shower it with Mills bombs, four each for six men. This would either destroy it outright, or cause at least some noise and confusion. No matter the direct outcome, the Germans would not retain a post at that location. Both sides followed a doctrine of re-sighting posts once they are known to be known. Daylight didn't bother Belfry so much, if it weren't for the sunrise, he might never have found the place. Right where everything was supposed to be, he directed the men to the positions as they'd practised them the night before. Down into this particular crater, wide and deep enough to hide them from sight, Belfry's men, Whitecroft and Corporal Cranliegh moving to the edge closest to the target; they would throw first. The Six Platoon men were to cover them, and then throw their own bombs after the first team fell back.

Finally, Belfry and his other man, Leland, would toss and lead the way home. Done right, this would create a frenzy of twenty four grenades being unleashed at one spot in a matter of seconds. Moving his eyes from one of his party to the next, all were in place, Belfry nodded to Cranliegh. Whitecroft peeked above the hummock, loosening the safety pin as he made himself ready to throw. All around the post was a collection of *Fieldgrau*. It shocked him so, he ducked back down.

"They're changing up, dozens of 'em." Belfry stepped forward.

"So? Throw and we'll get out of here."

"Did you release the lever on that?" asked Cranliegh.

"What?" Was Whitecroft's final response. The flash of explosive and smut of steel shards erased Whitecroft and Cranliegh in an instant, Belfry tumbled off his feet mid-step. Ear-ringing silence followed, each man left with his senses attempted to maintain sensibility. Pippin found himself staring at the sky.

"Who's hit?" Ferguson called out.

"I'm alright." Pippin was surprised to say. Belfry had landed on Leland, who was slow getting up. None of them heard the distant, but certain call of

"Achtung!" coming from the post. In a moment, Ferguson was at the berm, slick with remained of Cranliegh and Whitecroft.

"Shit! Here they come!" He reported, sliding back down into cover. Leland had at least gotten to his knees and was hauling the Sergeant to a seating position.

"How is he?"

"Alive, but bad hurt, man." Trickles of blood were seeping through several perforations in his tunic, his head lolled, more blood flowed from his ears, but the worst was the shredded stump of what had been his left leg.

"Can we move him?" asked Ferguson.

"He's awful heavy."

"They'll be here any second."

"Drop his rifle; and your bombs, get 'im by the arms and drag him back, I'll be right behind ye."

"What, Squeak?"

"You heard, Fern, get!"

"No way."

Pippin had a bomb to hand, "No time, Fern. Youse two are bigger than me- I can't help with the Sarge; but I can give you a head start." He yanked the pin, while Leland and Ferguson wrestled with Sergeant Belfry's inert form, starting back towards friendly lines as quickly as they could manage with so much dead weight.

"We brought Belfry in through the Two-Eightieth. He'll lose the leg if he lives. God knows what Squeak was doing while Leland and I got away, but it was a terrific racket. Didn't hear it after too long."

"Why'd you take him?"

"Squeak? He volunteered."

"He volunteers for everything."

"No reason to say no."

"No reason to not want him to come to harm." This had Ferguson to his feet, offended.

"I've just told you that he gave himself up to let us get away, and you want to make that my fault?"

Felix stood to meet his friend eye to eye while he drew out his trench knife, a gnarly affair with a serrated back and a knuckle duster grip. Without malice, but certainly not chummy, he rested the blade's tip on Ferguson's belt buckle.

"It's very convenient. Puts you in the clear of a few things with him out of the way."

"Squeak? What could I have against him? He's quite possibly the least offensive man of my recent acquaintance, which is a lot more that can be said for you, right now. If you're going to stick me, tell me why and put your weight behind it. If not, let me get along."

"He saw you shoot Collier."

"That madman? He wanted shooting, the nut." This was rather more a directness than Felix had thought would be forthcoming.

"Squeak said you popped him in the back. What was it, you owe him money, sleep with his sister?"

"Never saw him before that night. Hadn't a clue he was doolally until it was just me and him, at the first sally port we found. I tell you about it, you'll want to take that ribbon down and give it to me. You wouldn't have been alive to earn it if I hadn't dropped him. None of us would."

Wordlessly, Collier motioned for Pippin to stay put, tugged at Ferguson's sleeve and moved off into that low fold of ground. Moments crept by in slow tense movements until the both of them were at the foot of the German wire. Ferguson's recollection halted- it hadn't been wordless. Once putting Squeak in place, Collier had tugged his sleeve and whispered, quickly, full of moist breath, almost inaudible despite being directly in his ear, but was a defeated tone, resigned: "Has to be done." Ferguson would have only minutes to wonder about what he meant, if not only a strange choice of words.

Fancy him forgetting that, the first instance of there being something not quite right about the young officer. Compared with what those few minutes would contain, no wonder it seemed benign to him. How much did he need to tell Felix? He'd do his best to economise truth, after all, wasn't his 'friend' a knife's blade away at the moment? Aside from a small unsettling notion about the man he was working with, when they had approached this section of wire, he'd had a moment of relief. In a wonderful illusion, the defile through the German wire appeared as a series of unbroken webs of iron strands. Looked at slightly cock-eyed revealed that the lay of the ground was confusing the eye and a dog-legged path was traced through gaps which perspective forced to seem as if it were overlapping. Once he saw it, Ferguson couldn't view it any other way, but so cleverly was it done, he tried to will himself to see it in its deceptive form again. This could be a Godsend, he had thought, finding something so closely suited to purpose might mean an early night, and that suited him just fine. Surely the plumes of their frosty breath must be like smoke signals, even the smallest movement or tiny noise seemed amplified beyond reason and his heart climbed his throat, incrementally with each moment stalled at not much more than a wide open front door, only missing the mat saying "*Wilkommen.*" From that, with no consideration to the immediate situation, his thoughts flitted as to whether or not a door mat placed here would be in German. It would be much more neighbourly if it were to say "Welcome", he decided, quickly, regaining the gravity of the moment.

"Here," Collier had whispered, "here is good." It was, Ferguson had to agree, the best of its kind he'd ever seen, silently hoping the officer would make a note of it so they could get on with the rest of it.

"Right," he had then said, "you and me, up that hill and into them." It had been a statement so baffling, Ferguson was at first certain it was a very badly timed joke. Until, that was, he noticed Collier had drawn his pistol, levelling it in Ferguson's general direction.

"I'll not tell you again, lad, we're going up there."

"We'll be killed, Sir, all of us. We're only here to look for-"

"Wrong. The both of us are going to die today. Me, up there, you, down here, it doesn't matter." In a moment while he contemplated the route he had set for himself, Collier took both eyes off Ferguson, and inattentively let the muzzle of his .45 slip from keeping him in check. There was a split moment to decide; and hopefully a lifetime to deal with it. Almost as if the rifle went off on its own, Ferguson didn't remember sending out to his limbs the signal to adopt the standing fire position, the stock braced in the meat of the shoulder, the tiny flex of finger, a disproportionate movement considering the result- the trigger released the hammer, which struck the pin, sparking the primer and igniting the charge. He couldn't remember hearing the shot; it was certain that Collier didn't hear it either, and he hit the frozen mud of that February night seemingly without noise, but it was the shock of the shot which had overridden Ferguson's ability to detect sound. All that had been left was to make sure he hadn't got the whole patrol killed while trying to prevent getting the whole patrol killed.

"If you were there, you'd have done it yourself." There was little Ferguson could say about this whole mess with more sureness than that. "It'd be all over and done with if you weren't still pissed about having to go after those maps."

Attempting a deliberate coolness, Felix tapped the knife's tip twice on Fern's buckle before sheathing it, unblooded, without breaking eye with the other man.

"You've said your bit. If you believe it, that's now between you and nobody else; which seems to suit you not having to answer for anything. In the meantime, I'm getting you out of my Section." He threw his jacket on but didn't get far towards the Platoon tent to lay protest.

"Thorncliffe just made me your 2 I/C."

"What?" Felix turned to face his erstwhile friend.

"The Bulldog was up for it, said he didn't want it."

Nobody had sold Felix on any of this when he signed on. Reflecting on that brought forward all the nuances of his life which hadn't been part of the pitch. He hadn't really believed, at the start anyway, that he could possibly come to harm. So many things, wishful thinking, fantasy, and absolutes of all sorts had been proven to be misleading at the top end to verifiable destruction of truth all the way at the bottom. Very slim was the hope that Squeak was due to appear, an eventuality diminishing as the sun set. This was nothing of right and wrong, motive made no difference to outcome. Allowing Squeak to go into danger because he was the right one to do the job, or by having him gone left Fern alone to his conscience, the man was lost. It didn't matter, but he wished desperately that it did, not even caring which way, because maybe if he could have it mean something it might seem a little less unfair.

That fucking telegram.

"He was going home, Andy, d'ye know that? They were sending him home."

It wasn't quite the right shape, and a little heavier, but with the right wind up, Pippin could loft a Mills bomb like returning a caught fly to the mound. His first toss cleared the shattered trees, the lever departing mid-flight in a metallic pop which set the fuse. A moment of nothing hung within the lightening mist. The grenade boomed, raising a geyser of clotted mud and shrapnel. As soon as that happened, Pippin rushed the forward edge of the berm, mechanically cranking shot after shot from his rifle. He wasn't a good shot, and knew it, but his effort had no basis in marksmanship. Each time he fired, he moved the muzzle exaggeratedly to the left or right, or shifted his own position, trying to confound and slow up the Boshes rather than picking them off. Pippin wasn't even too sure where the enemy were. Once or twice, the sharp song of passing bullets let him know they were getting closer. He chanced a rearward look and couldn't see his mates, perhaps they'd indeed gotten away. Closing the bolt on an empty chamber, the hollow click of hammer against nothing alerted him that he'd shot his lot. Instead of reloading, he dropped the weapon and came back down into defilade, tossing his second bomb as he did so, as close as he dared to his post. Where Belfry had landed was the Sergeant's abandoned rifle and a clutch of Mills bombs like iron eggs. Without stopping, Pippin grabbed the Enfield and another bomb, casually rolling it down into the dead ground as he broke cover and crested the rearward bank.

Three Germans rushed the now deserted throwing point, and never had a chance to see the collection of grenades which all went off as one, leaving them in the same distributed mess as Whitecroft and Cranliegh. Their comrades were more circumspect, and after the explosion, skirted the edges of low ground, two on either side. Pippin had only moved back a handful of yards, getting behind a tree stump and hazarding another shot. It struck, to his amazement, the German closest to him; the man slumping forward. I got one! He told himself, immensely pleased, but didn't linger as the remaining Germans were hot on his heels. It was time he wasn't here, he thought, and leapt up to take another bound, just another few yards to the next fold in the earth. A heavy punch hit him, near his shoulder. It was so hard, it caused him to misstep a little; harder than anytime David had hit him. David, five years older, had been, from time to time, a brutish thug whose favourite abuse was to haul off and hit his younger sibling in such a fashion as to cause a leg or arm to shortly go numb. This had been much the same, but worse on a greater magnitude. All this rushing about had winded him so, and without really knowing why, he lay down to try and catch his breath. When he did, he was unaware that it was his last.

Chapter XVIII

France, April, 1917.

Many months ago, the Commander-in-Chief came to an agreement with his French confederate about the overall plan for offensive operations in 1917. At each step on the way through the levels of martial structure, plans were formed, reviewed, reformed and broken down to pass along to subordinate units. Generals and colonels had all had their hands to it and now these details, much diluted had come down a long narrowing path to the penultimate level. All through the night before, after Captain McCormack had held conference with his platoon commanders, Lieutenant Thorncliffe had taken the notes pertaining to him and reworked them specific to his men. This morning, though they had known in a broad sense what their jobs would be, Six Platoon would be hearing the specifics. Sweeny, his batman, had set up the beach chair under a yawning tree. There were a few minutes before his section commanders brought the men over. Just a few minutes to fret as to whether or not anything had been left to chance, or overlooked. Of course, his forgetfulness was one thing, and couldn't account for anything omitted by Captain McCormack or Field Marshall Haig and every step on the way in between the two.

Patrick Desmond Thorncliffe needn't have been worried, about his part, anyway, he'd always had a meticulousness for detail. That had certainly helped him in getting his degree awarded with honours. Not as if he had any practical idea of what to do with a background in Classics. He didn't much care about it as a course of study with any passion. The agreement had been that Paddy would go to university, a level of education the elder Mister Thorncliffe had missed. From the agreement came the argument. If his dad had come up through hard work and frugality, why was uni so important to a good life? On the other hand, from the comfort he grew up in because of that quality in his father, what did he know at that age about hard work and frugality? If school would keep the peace between them, Paddy would tow the line, in spirit at least, but he determined to study an area that his father couldn't see any value in. This choice had his dad apoplectic.

"Our boy just isn't swift enough to realise he should have read law; that we he could argue for a living." Paddy was "contrary" and "wilful", qualities both men despised in others despite cherishing it in themselves. Several times he'd wanted to chuck it in altogether, but dad wouldn't have it. War had re-ignited the debate between father and son. Once again, Paddy was refused, worse, he was forbidden to join up unless he finished his degree. Determination set in, and if he had to do it, he was going to do it right, hence the honours. At the time he wasn't aware how well that attitude would serve his first professional endeavour, and he was no further along with what to do with himself beyond all this. Pragmatically, he'd have to get beyond all of this first; the rest would follow. As such, pragmatism was best applied sparingly, lest it lead to despondency. For three years they had been at this, and they still hadn't left France yet. Never mind Tipperary, it was a long bloody way to Berlin.

A platoon commander had the privilege of knowing each man under him individually, an intimacy not found at higher levels of command. Some, he knew more well than others, but only based on how long an individual had been with the platoon. The number of them who had been with him all this way so far may have waned in place of reinforcements, Thorncliffe still made his thoroughness work well for him. Applied here it took the form of a one-on-one chat with every man at the first prudent instant when they came to his platoon. He had yet to miss this once even though to his recollection, some of these interviews seemed to last longer than a man's tenure under his command. Thorncliffe wasn't counting Collier in that, but not deliberately, that lad had come and gone while he'd been away. Shame, really. Thorncliffe really enjoyed this aspect of his job, getting to know new people, and Collier may have been worth getting to know. Funny how it seemed sometimes, a man could have the worst, last experience of his life and no one would be able to say anything singular about them. Status as an officer kept him socially apart from the other ranks, making for a decidedly complex relationship. His interactions with the men had to be decidedly paternalistic, an aggregate of concern and aloofness, which could be a difficult aim when most of the men were his age or older. In training to become an officer, he had clung to one important thing. Because he could have such close knowledge of his men, he had opportunity to build something which would be superlative. The platoon, he'd been told, is the unit in the attack. Placing a definite article there was all his headstrong leanings needed to hear. As with most things, this would be give and take. Thorncliffe could only groom a sharp and effective outfit if he was the best of them all. It fell to him to set the example, in attitude and competence and demand a high standard on all occasions from his men; and one could not be present without the other. This wasn't instinct, it had begun with his introduction to the Regiment, which had been September of 1915, at Niagara when he'd been invited, with all the other prospective platoon commanders to the plush lounge of the riverside inn Sinclair had made his headquarters.

The steep bank on the opposite shore to the inn was coated in whiskers of tenacious scrub, rooted through fissures, rising with flatly layered shale, climbing to great heights, creating an uneven tier of trees. Most were full of verdant late summer glory, though now that was being slowly overtaken by flashes, match heads of bright radiance soon to catch the entire escarpment in autumn's fire. This made for a sleepy afternoon wanting to pull lidded eyes to the dusty light of open windows and the show of nature outside. Sixteen young men were grouped around richly lacquered tables, too distantly tired and strange to one another for conversation to drown the creak of the inn's mill wheel turning by the tumble of a little run of river or the repeating call of cardinals.

Some men had been in camp for a few days longer than the others, but all had spent at least one night under canvas. A new experience in living rough coupled to what was for most a long journey in getting to Niagara could only work as an excuse to fatigue and a crumpled appearance at this early stage and no further. No two amongst them were entirely dressed alike. Some had uniforms, from Officer Training Corps with their universities, from a rare selection of commissioned Militia men coming to active service rather late and not a few men who had already been drilling as privates for the week or so before. These were men who'd attested for overseas service and administrative checks had discovered the appropriate qualifications for a King's Commission. Men in plain clothes, easily marked as the most recent arrivals for the most part had applied to their school's OTC for commissioned service, though they may not have paraded with the Corps at any point previously. All had been brought here, to this room, on the invitation of Lieutenant Colonel Barclay Archibald Sinclair, DSO. He appeared before them and outshone all present in his finery. His well-tailored jacket sat firmly over broad shoulders and expertly concealed the spread of weight around his midriff which hadn't been there fifteen years ago. Brass was so highly polished that shoulder badges and tunic buttons caught sunlight as he turned or moved, emitting sparks of blinding shine. The Glengarry atop his head, with a green and white checkered band sported the Regimental badge he'd designed- the Sinclair rooster imposed over a motif of maple leaf and Scots' saltire; echoing in picture the Gaelic mottos underneath, *"Aonan Righ Dà Dūthchanan"*- One King Two Countries. The hat itself was cocked so rakishly that the peak of its front met his right eyebrow. The kilt, of the Hunting Sinclair tartan, was his own; he'd had it for ages and had it let out as need be over the years. Some wags said Sinclair had chosen his family tartan to save himself the price of a kilt, but that would be disregarding the wealthy retailer having personally funded the Regimental accoutrement that went beyond government issue. Being of a long age of wear, the kilt's slight fade dimmed the tartan to a washed, deep green, but brought out the shine of the black leather sporran and contrasted with that piece's sequence of blonde horse hair tassels.

Sinclair, his purpose in appearance to be as impressive to these young men as he could had opted to mount his medals above his left breast as opposed to the coloured ribbons which were more usual for day-to-day. These shone as well, but dazzled more by what they represented rather than physical lustre. His Distinguished Service Order took precedence, accented by both the Queen's and the King's South Africa Medals, the row summed up with the Colonial Auxiliary Forces Officer's Decoration and the North West Campaign Medal he'd earned during that rebellion when he himself was a subaltern, which was before some of those he was about to address had been born.

At the urging of those who had a sense of propriety, the sixteen potential platoon commanders stood as he entered. Taking his place before them all he cast eyes upon each, a sumptuary evaluation, before he spoke.

"Be seated," he waited for them to settle before he continued. "Good afternoon, Gentlemen. Foremost for me to explain to you now is that title; 'Gentlemen', is what you all are or are about to become. Those of you who already hold a King's Commission should be aware of the tremendous authority bestowed upon you. It quite literally means that in the absence of His Majesty in the field you are a lawful representative of his sovereignty. Which is precisely why you young men <u>must</u> be gentlemen, as your actions are in fact required to be an emulation of His Majesty and thus must be of the highest standards.

"These standards, thankfully, are illustrated in detail within the King's Regulation and Orders. Being inconvenient to consult these volumes at short notice, I shall put to your mind what you should strive for in keeping with the principles of being an officer in one word: Cleanliness.

"It has been said that a gentleman will keep himself irreproachable in his conduct; in his manners, his language and the care of his person. Cleanliness, in all of these at all times is what I expect from you, strictly because those placed above my command expect the same from me. You all need to uphold such a nature of purpose as that is the only way by which you may successfully discharge your duties.

As officers, these responsibilities are twofold. In both, without though to personal desire, comfort and safety, you will carry out the orders and directions of your superiors while also being worthy of the leadership of those placed under your command through any circumstance of hardship, danger or despair. His Majesty chose carefully the words of the commissions he grants. The King, Gentlemen, is Trusting and Confident in your personal Loyalty, Courage and Good Conduct. Any one of you failing in this trust will cause me to fail in mine. I shall not permit this. You had better be beyond my mortal reach before you permit it in yourself."

Sinclair paused, to let the message take hold.

"Cleanliness, at all times, in all things. Keep that in mind, and you shall do well. That's it, Gentlemen. Report to your Company Commanders in five minutes' time. Dismissed."

Thorncliffe had always done his best to abide by that single watch-word, which proved more difficult with the passage of time in a world descending ever more steeply into filthiness, physically, morally, spiritually.

Chapter XIX

Like wraiths on such a cool bright morning, the men were coming in for the big chat through the trees of Sheepy Baa Woods to the small glade where Thorncliffe was to hold court.

"Gather in, close as you can." The preparatory bombardment was in full swing. In the last week of March it had begun, but with only half of all guns firing at any one time. This had been purposeful fire, seeking out enemy gun pits and rearward positions of interest, rail heads, marshalling yards, supply dumps, while only revealing half of their own potential. Three days ago, the artillery's final preparation began with all guns continuously barking forth, shattering wire and keeping Fritz right where he was. Their front line troops, by the time they were met face to face, will have been under fire, in their dugouts, tossed as on a rough sea from the persistent concussion, starved and thirsty for want of supplies that could not reach them. Their word for this constant shelling before a big attack was "*Trammelfuhr*"-drumfire. Knocked about so thoroughly for seven days on end, perhaps they may be disinclined to the coming fight. None too likely, as, proud men themselves, it was a high mark of esteem for them to endure the unendurable. They could be expected to give their very best, even after a week-long trouncing. The noise was tremendous; invisible packages of doom tearing overhead so the platoon crowding in was an aid against Thorncliffe having to repeat himself.

"Spark 'em up if you want." Matches scraped and lighters blossomed, the gallery of seated men before him obscured by the number of simultaneous first puffs. "Troops, orders. We got some army stuff to go over, but we'll get into the goods in due course." He smiled, all part of the confidence act of leadership, flipped his notebook open and went right into it.

"The Canadian Corps, acting in conjunction with the rest of the First Army on the South and Third Army WILL attack and consolidate the Enemy's positions, penetrating to a depth of from one thousand to two thousand yards. One more time..." Thorncliffe repeated the mission statement verbatim, the custom of ensuring that all understood the definite nature. They were not attempting, they were accomplishing. Formality out of the way, he relaxed his posture, from however rigid it might have been, reposed in that striped canvas sling he was so fond of. "Alright, lads. That's the big picture. Here's how it looks for us. Sweeny, the first hand-out, please." A stack of mimeographed sheets was distributed out, one for each man. It was a simplified thumbnail of the ground 'B' Company would cover. Captain McCormack had spent a great deal of effort in detail of design and it was immediately understandable to most of the men. Habit being what it was, the Captain had spent so long at his draft, when he gave his orders late last night he reeked dangerously of whiskey and strong coffee.

Thorncliffe continued once everyone had their page. "Study these, put them to memory. We won't have them to work with on the day. You see, it's a general advance. Buckshee has 'A' on the left and 'D' on the right. Our Company flanks are solid. Well, as solid as those yahoos of 'inAction' and 'Disaster' can be. In the advance, Five Platoon ties in with 'A' and Eight with 'D'. Which leaves us, boys, comforted by mates on all sides, as we go after the plum.

"Six Platoon <u>WILL</u> advance in keeping with the covering barrage to our objective along the Red Line- the enemy machine gun redoubt at 'Castle Switch'. We will destroy this position and form a strongpoint on the ground held once we consolidate. The next wave will pass through as the barrage shifts to take their objectives downslope along the Black Line. Our assault, and the waves following are dependent on moving with the barrage. This puts us on a precise schedule. We must be in possession of Castle Switch, in strength, within forty minutes of zero hour." A ripple of consternation went through the audience. "Look, each platoon in this company has had a go at the mock up, in all positions. The Captain had to pick the right men for the task, and he knew to rely on us. And let me tell you, Fritz won't know what hit him. All that noise above is landing on his head and will continue 'till we go over. He's a sharp chap, our Fritz. He'll be ready to get at his guns once we're ready to step off. What he won't expect is how close we'll be. Six Platoon is going to deploy from a sap cut eighty yards ahead of our current front line. They'll still be cowed and scattered from the bombardment and we'll go into them with bombs and steel before they're given a chance.

"What we gain, we are to hold. Nobody is permitted to withdraw from a position without being ordered to do so. Moving with the second wave will be carrying parties and stretcher bearers. The parties will drop wire, tools and extra ammunition to help us build our consolidated position. Stretcher bearers alone will attend the wounded. Maximum speed and aggression on the advance means we stop for nothing. At that time we'll be taking delivery of one of the Battalion MG's. Let's hope that goes better than the last time. Sweeny, hand-out number two, please." This was a diagram on tighter scale than the last, and Thorncliffe's artistic contribution. Each man, noted as a circle or square was placed as they were to be, the whole broken down into four steps, as a dance, sections moving through each to their own choreography, according to purpose. Thorncliffe was one of only a few subalterns in the King's Own whose chain of command below him- despite shifts in organisation and the departure of men- could reach back to original members of his platoon. Three out of four section commanders were only recent 'chosen men', though all could claim presence at First Muster. Untested by command under fire and directing troops of disparate levels of experience, Thorncliffe had to trust in the confidence of these new NCO's, and his confidence in them.

"One Section."

"Sir," Strachan answered. Felix Strachan certainly had not been given a section by happenstance. The man was infuriatingly cheeky;

more prone to give a smart answer than the correct one. Strachan's grace was that he usually knew the right answer. It appeared more endearing once that was discovered, rather than obstinacy. This in itself became a wit-inspired charisma backed up by a swift mind, telling qualities of a good officer, but Strachan lacked much in reading and arithmetic. A product of a one room schoolhouse and whatever lessons his mother could cram into him besides, he had left just after the first semester of the tenth grade to take up the work on his uncle's estate other hands had abandoned for the cause. A truncated scholastic career wasn't to blame any more so than his intellect for not having a solid grounding in essentials. In actuality, it was a dreaminess, inspired by boredom. His mind thirsted so much for a challenge of more complexity, it left the building during the basics, only to return to be confounded by a complex challenge when it appeared because he'd been mentally absent for the little things he needed to know to resolve it.

"You will be first in order of advance, forming up to the front of Platoon HQ in Artillery Formation. When the pre-sited marker 'Flagstaff' is reached-you will give the signal by calling 'Flagstaff' and blowing your whistle. The Platoon will move to Assault Formation, your men will form up line abreast to the front and left. As the Platoon comes to the next marker 'Pivot Stumps', shift your section left oblique and put enfilade fire along the enemy front line trench. This is your Assault Position. You will gain lodgement in this trench and clear towards MG Number One, directly after Three Section's second volley of rifle bombs. On consolidation, Two Section will be on your right, a section from Five Platoon will be on your left."

Thorncliffe turned to Ellins, who had been another easy choice to take on a section. Like Strachan, he was a swift mind though a bit more certain of it. That boy knew a lot of stuff and wasn't shy about sharing a vast minutia of fact. It was all well-chosen from a wealth of everything he'd ever read having stuck fast, seldom irrelevant or lacking interest. Ellins' delivery could be a tiresome if mistaken his confidence in knowledge as an air of grandeur. Two Section, the Bombing Section, as Thorncliffe explained, were to parallel One Section, gaining the right had trench and assaulting MG Number Two. A deep dugout, sheltering the defenders was along this stretch and Ellins' bombers had that added to their task list.

Sutherland's Section, the Rifle Bombers, had been equipped and rehearsed on their devices, the man in charge a graduate of a rifle bomb course. Every one of them had tested live on the projector, none had had any instance to fire in earnest. Of all his assets, Three Section was Thorncliffe's biggest unknown. Given the shortened distance of open ground the Platoon was to cover from the sap entrance, Sutherland's men would fire only two volleys. Once as soon as they cleared the sap, the second after passing the first marker 'Flagstaff'. At the next marker, they would fire at will until One and Two Sections rushed the trench. Keeping their part as simple as this worked against uncertainty.

Thorncliffe had entrusted his last section, Four Section, to Corporal Tapscott. He had been made a section commander very early on, and now Tapscott was the last of Six Platoon's first junior NCO's to remain in place. The Lewis Gun Section was wrapped around the nucleus of Atherton and Robbins and their weapon. The rest of the section were riflemen kitted out with rigged-up aprons to haul the supply of ammo for the gun. Atherton and Robbins were some of the most dependable men Thorncliffe had, and were well practised, the former given a stripe in recognition of his part at Goose Egg Crater. With such a veteran core, there had been no concern with placing the lion's share of the reinforcements under Tapscott's tutelage. If he lasted the day, he was due his third stripe and thence would be bound to fill a Sergeant's vacancy, a cautiously hedged bet. Four Section would only go so far as 'Pivot Stumps' from where they would put fire on the German casements, lifting fire, as with Three Section upon the assault.

One and Two Sections would signal with flares once their objectives were taken and contact made with the flanks. These flares indicated for Platoon HQ, Three and Four Section to move forward to begin consolidation. Everything was reliant on speed. The assaulting sections were not to fire on the move, but to establish themselves in their final positions without stopping, laying down controlled and directed fire on target before taking the German trench.

"Reports on prisoners taken in recent raids is that the section of line we are taking is held by an under-strength platoon of the Nine-Thirty-second Reserve Infantry Regiment- 'Herzog-Heinrich Regiment'. These boys are Bavarians; some might have even been at Spoon Farm. We got the best of them then, and we are better than we ever were now." Of course, Spoon Farm had been anything but a walk over. While Thorncliffe could take credit for his part, with a genuine humility, he owed a lot to Douglas. Poor old Merrick had his chips without opportunity to contribute. Douglas had been lucky enough in living through that awful opening, and followed that up with a consistency in a fight and out of the line. Six Platoon was as much the Sergeant's as it was his, though Douglas always deferred professionally to the Lieutenant. They had worked this bunch into a team together, looked after them, had seen altogether too many carried off the field. Even though Basil Douglas and Paddy Thorncliffe were only on the most infrequent familiarity of a first name basis they would miss each other more than any man in the Platoon should either one be taken away. Thorncliffe, unknown to the Sergeant, had gone to bat, all the way to Sinclair to forestall Douglas' advancement. McCormack recommended Douglas be appointed Sergeant-Major at the next opening, while the Colonel thought he'd suit a field commission. Thorncliffe couldn't halt that indefinitely; if Sinclair said so, that's all there was, and as important as Sergeant Douglas had been, it wasn't right to keep him from his potential.

Drawing up his meeting, he looked out at the collection of faces; the personalities behind them. These were his men. In less than five days, they would all be gone. Either the battle would take them altogether, or piece by piece and would leave those who remained altered by the experience in ways impossible to predict. The new and old, experienced and novice, he was proud of what they had become. Lieutenant Thorncliffe was certain that they were all good at their jobs individually and in harmony. His founding belief above all was that they were all intrinsically good men. Of the newest men, Tremaine, or "Tremor" as he was fast becoming known, certainly was an interesting case in point. Thorncliffe knew, by way of his interview with him, the sideways fashion he had come to be a rifleman. To help fulfill the promise from on high to fill the troop order before the general offensive, service and support units had been canvassed for able men, along with replacements being rushed through training and returning wounded. Tremaine was here of his own volition, which was admirable. That he had also taken all the Bull Ring could spit at him was positively praiseworthy; a man so practically skeletal as to have a permanently famished look about him, a uniform slightly too large seemed he may have been disappearing into himself. The kilt he'd been issued only served to showcase knobby knees separated by a bowed stance of a lifetime riding. As he'd brought some of his trade's tools, Tremaine had enterprisingly set himself up, with Thorncliffe's permission and by his wheedling Company Stores for a supply of tacks, in re-soling the men's boots, twenty-five cents a pair. He worked without anvil or mount, bracing the leather with those blanched stems of his, keeping his hands free to fly about, pulling stripped tacks and driving fresh ones home in a deft and singular rhythm. While he may have looked like a stiff breeze could blow him away, there was nothing shaky about him. Between himself and the Lieutenant, five cents from each job went into the Platoon kitty, a fund managed by Sweeny, which would go towards "free" issues of drink when in rest billets.

"Well, that's it. In a little while we're going to move out to the training ground and work on what we just went over. Let's look sharp at this. We've been given a hard job, but by God we're going to do it with style." The men stirred, milled about, forming small groups of whoever had been sitting nearby to discuss their thoughts on the plan.

"Why is it always the Bavarians?" Felix asked Bert, in a rhetorical way that the other was sure to miss.

"Rather them than Prussians."

"What's wrong with Prussians?" This was from Drummond, one of the reinforcements given to Ellins' section, who was listening in on the corporals with Fielding, another new man.

"Wha's wrang with them?" Felix chortled, "The whole lot are nasty wee de'ils. You can't blame them, when it's us they have to fight."

"On a sliding scale though," Ellins clarified.

"In that case, I'd rather it were Bavarians," Felix opined. Drummond kept hearing "barbarians" and was a little unsettled. "Prussians are taking this thing way too seriously."

"Yep. Who do you think is in charge over there if it's not the Prussians? It was they who invented the notion of a modern standing army of professionals."

"When was that?"

"Sixteen Forty-four."

"I'll take your word on it. At least Bavarians have a sense of humour. D'you remember, Bert, that time with the Stokes?" Not too long ago, but before the arrival of Drummond and Fielding, a trench mortar crew had arrived in the platoon's front line position for a spot of harassing fire. They lobbed ugly looking bombs from the Stokes pattern mortar towards the German line, with little thought to accuracy. Trench mortar teams were reviled because every time they put a few shots out, Fritz would have to get his own back, but usually after the mortar men had made tracks. They had waited for the retaliation, in tense minutes of expecting the world to collapse. They were answered, but in a way no one expected. Opposite a sign was being held aloft. "Nice Try, Canada," it read on one side, "but the score is still 3-2."

"We'll tie it up Monday. It'll be a dawdle," Felix started, but the lie didn't sit well. "Really, I can't tell you what it will be like. The best that can be hoped for is that as few things as possible go wrong."

"And the worst?" Fielding asked with a bit of glass half-empty. Felix shrugged.

"Won't mean a thing to get hung up on that. Worst happens, we none of us will be around to complain about it." What he was failing at was describing an experience so mortally personal no one who'd had it could adequately explain to anyone else. Therefore, he could only go so far to prepare men like Drummond and Fielding, or come to that, himself.

"It is good that war is so terrible-"

"Napoleon again, Bert?"

"No, Catscratch, Robert E Lee." Felix had heard the name, but couldn't place it. Lest Bert be thought the cleverer of the two corporals, he tried to nod sagely. Bert was beginning to learn that while he had a lot of bright things to say, it was wise to be quick about it. The talk had moved on from his last bon mot, and he'd not told them the second part of Lee's succinct observance. It wouldn't be too long before all of them would know what Bobby Lee had been driving at, so he left it there, unsaid.

Chapter XX

Church Parade was usual on a Sunday out of the line. When that day was spent in trenches, Major McCowan did his best to get out to as many men that he could. This Sunday was altogether far too important in so many ways to leave it to chance. McCowan had insisted to Sinclair he be allowed to deliver a sermon. The Colonel had gone so far as handing over the Battalion's Advanced Headquarters, which could hold a company at a time. As each one came in turn to the ruined church, they paused and McCowan delivered his Easter message. They would then be directed towards the final positions, shelters, trenches and tunnels where they would jump off from early the next morning. Before this, each man going forward came through Petit Rejour, the old path winding past St Gertrude, past Pere Lejune standing in the shadow of the Saint's statue, giving benediction with one hand, the other clutching his rosary. Beads of wood, symbolising his poverty had been worn to a dull shine in a record of devoted piety. His gaze remained skyward, so that the tears fell from bleary eyes. The rector was old enough to have memory of the last war, when he was only a curate. Another age ago, it was much the same, in cause at least. Men had been misdirected by the powerful to go against values claimed to be sacred only for the earthly gain of the powerful. Once again, he had seen his countrymen, rushing to the sound of the guns, and repulsed, only to return and stay when the front stabilised. They were now a memory, some of them resting in the stone fenced yard. It was *les Anglais* next, which Pere Lejune had a personal crisis with. Gervais Lejune had been raised by a generation who mistrusted, derided, hated and fought the English. Very few shared the same method of faith as he, and his ability to communicate with any of them was strained by his faltering grasp of English and their near universal lack of French. It took a great deal of contrition to accept they were here for the protection of his parish; that they too were dying in great numbers in the effort. If he could, as he came to be able, embrace them in all difference, it challenged his perspective on *les Allemandes*. All men, misdirected by the powerful, they all could be forgiven; and blessed for the courage they showed while chained to their fate. Men of the King's Own passing him now, in their serried company ranks were both purposeful, heels digging the road in a solid cadence and resigned, shoulders drawn forward, chins to chest. None would be returning, they were '*en avant*', pledging they would not be turned back. No, not this time. Pere Lejune, weeping as they went by, prayed for them, he prayed for all of them: the living, the dead and those about to die; on either side. He prayed that the powerful could be forgiven their ambition.

Major McCowan also held himself in prayer as a Company would start crowding in.

"Jock," Colonel Sinclair had instructed him, "you've got to do this four times on a tight timetable. Make it a gem, but for goodness sake, keep it brief." May his words be a guide and comfort, was his appeal. Angry winds were flirting with thick, rolling clouds. Very little daylight peeked through, the constant rattle and gusty tear of a spectacular bombardment travelling above, not impeded in the least by the gathering storm. Battalion Advance Headquarters would shortly no longer be here, abandoning this place as it had been found, collapsing, neglected long before the war. Pere

Lejune knew it as the fist St Gertrude's, disused since his grandfather's time, when the railway and industry began to pull the farmers away from the outskirts, concentrating with others seeking fortune and an easier life. This was the migration which made Petit Rejour the idyll French village it had once been; what it hoped to be again, someday.

Properly, then, *Sainte Gertrude l'Ancienne* had been quietly going to pieces on its own for a tick over a century. Large areas of the roof had collapsed inward from rotting timber joists, the mortar between the stones was decaying, adding occasional oblong slabs to navigate. Above, missing portions of what had been a good attempt at a vaulted ceiling showed the broiling, tumbling clouds; dirty greys, shadows of black, never revealing any promise of fair treatment filled the voids as a moving fresco, alive with menace.

"It is usual for me to discuss the great Miracle and Promise that is Easter Sunday. I needn't tell you," the Reverend looked out upon the khaki ranks of his congregation jostled into the interrupted floor space of the ruined stone church, "that this is an unusual time. Tomorrow, we will be expected to do our duty. It might even mean the taking of life, or the giving of our own lives. We may be afraid of these things, and rightly so. No better man than any of us hasn't faced his own mortality or the consequence of breaking natural law. Now, just because we are all equal in this fear does not mean it should be the equal of us. Oh, no. Particularly as soldiers we know about a desperate fear- of the uncontrollable, the unknown- and yet we go into battle and win our victories. Why is this so? My friends, the very entity to which we belong provides the answer. Each of us knows what they are to do and precisely who is in authority over us as much as those we may lead ourselves. This is a very long line, indeed; which must come to an ultimate end, hmm?

"Our Lord provides this, in the story where He has come from teaching on the Mount, to Capernaum. We take our lesson from Matthew, Chapter Eight, verses Five to Thirteen." There was a rustling wave as those who had them, brought out their pocket bibles and thumbed to the right page. "It concerns a Centurion- a military man who represented Rome's occupation. Think of him as a Company Commander. While he had a place in the structure of the Roman Legion, he had obligations to the people under his occupation as well. He would have collected taxes, by force if need be; but we also know that this Centurion built the synagogue for the people of Capernaum despite not being Jewish himself. As our Lord approached, messengers from the Centurion came and told Him of a sick servant.

"'Tell him I shall come and cure him,' said our Lord. The messengers went, but were soon back, saying that the Centurion knew he wasn't worthy to have our Lord as his guest, instead telling Him: 'Only speak the word, and my servant will be healed. For I also am a man under authority, with authority over others myself.' So impressed was our Lord that He at once healed the servant and declared the Centurion's faith greater than any He had seen in Israel.

"This faith, put in this particular way should seem familiar, my friends. It is not that our Lord would do what was asked of Him, but a faith in the certainty that if our Lord wills it; it shall be done. The Centurion's faith is in the understanding of authority and obedience- that the word of God is obeyed; his humility is in having no expectation in his desired outcome.

"Our Lord himself knew this to be true, as His betrayal and crucifixion had been foretold by God's Prophecy. His sacrifice was His obedience to this ultimate authority. This is the level of faith He praised the Centurion for, without reservation or expectation. Let us all take up such a faith, for with that as our shield, we shall fear naught. Why should we fear what is beyond mortal knowledge? The unknown or uncontrollable are only such to those who give no thought of omnipotence. If some of us may die tomorrow, may we, in our obedience of God's authority, die well.

"There will be no hymn. The lesson has ended, go to your duties."

All about, men refastened their fighting equipment and would shortly be taken forward to their staging areas. There was some lingering as they shook out. From here, the company's platoons would be going separate ways, and some time was allowed for good-byes. Major McCowan took this chance to greet as many of the congregation as limited time allowed. He shook hands with the crushing grip men of his work seemed inclined to, and shared a few words. He couldn't steal a moment with all of them, and so much he wanted to, for he was always afraid of leaving something unsaid.

"Felix! Felix, my boy," he shouted enthusiastically, the corporal's hand sinking into the vice of McCowan's bony hand. "A Happy Easter. You have everything you need? Any word from home?"

"Ah, yes, Padre. Got a letter from me Ma. Things are grand. Just grand."

"Oh, so pleased to hear."

There wasn't enough time to tell the Padre about it. The last mail call they'd had he'd got it, and only so quickly put it aside. Orders had been all personal letters and documents were to be left with their barracks kit. The envelope was heavier than usual, and as Felix tore it open a handsome gold lighter fell out into his hand. Plucking the cream stationary out, he read:

"My Dear Boy

Thank you for the pictures you and William sent. It is so good to see you both so well. You put me in mind so much of your Father, it breaks my heart every day you are gone. Had you forgotten to put that cigarette away before the photo was taken? The game's up on your smoking, son. Try not to let anything else come to harm you.

We've had a letter from James. He has been accepted to train with the Flying Corps. He said he will write you when he can. May God send you both back to me,

Your loving mother."

Felix had been relieved of his worry over his brother, to a degree. James' training would last far longer going in this direction, if it weren't any less dangerous. He was always a bit of an idiot, our James, he thought. Right now, he shifted from one foot to the other.

"I'm not sure I get what you were on about just now."

"What troubles you?"

"That I don't know if there's such a thing as dying well."

"Oh?"

"Dying well, I guess, means that there'd be such a thing as dying poorly."

"Yes, I would think so."

"Dead is dead, Padre. Why should one fellow be admired and the other pitied?"

"Ah, not saying that, Felix. It isn't about how you die which matters, it is in how you used the moments before, each one, mind, towards doing the right thing. Always do your best to do the next right thing, and you won't fear judgement upon your call to Glory. I hope to speak to you again soon." McCowan was off, spreading his message to other men. Put in that way, the Padre's concept was a bit more reasonable. Yet, Felix had spent a lot of time and thought on this question in terms of others; he'd not spent either to reflect personally. That was the conceit of mortality. As soon as one becomes aware of the finality of life, it is natural to conceive that as a far distant event, much more likely to happen to others. Such a protective concept was strained by the sheer volume of proof recently that, as he'd put it, "dead is dead." McCowan's gentle reminder was that same protection from fear found in the mind wishing to deny personal finality could be had in the soul being at peace for knowing that whenever it came, death would be taking a man who had done the best he could. A particular serenity surrounded that thought, but it was interrupted by Thorncliffe.

"Six Platoon, prepare to move. One Section up front."

"One Section, on your feet," his men were already standing; he turned away to face the guide who would take them forward, so the Section couldn't see the sheepish look that had descended on him.

"Let's go, chum," he said to his guide, who started forward. Felix, his section and the rest of Six Platoon stepped off behind.

Chapter XXI

Right up until a couple of weeks prior, none of Six Platoon had been down a mine. Whatever professional background they had, if any, it didn't include mining. All those chaps who'd joined up from the pits were more valuable digging holes in France to be made into riflemen. The work was certainly no less dangerous as not only did the perils of tunneling deep underground exist as it did at home, here there were people lethally determined to stop their progress. Concerns of time, manpower and secrecy had demanded what the sappers built meet certain bare standards of practicality. Sappers are not generally known for being satisfied with such a low bar. They consider themselves, correctly, as craftsman. Pride was evident in the placard at the entrance to the underground, declaring in bold, stencilled letters:

"Welcome to Schlump Subway,

Courtesy 2123 Tunnellers."

Each man in Six Platoon had been brought through over the last few days, to orient them with a place unlike any other they had seen, and weed out any who showed an inclination to panic in tight spaces. 'Schlump Subway' was only a channel towards the saps from which the infantry attack would commence, and had only been carved wide enough for two men to pass abreast, and then only if they obliged each other by approaching on an incline. A dampness surrounded every surface, penetrating the nose thickly. The men stifled sneezes and dripped snot. Glistening walls seemed softer than they were with the play of yellow electric bulbs adding dimensions of shade and light. These were spaced with each timber buttress, precisely ten yards apart. Fed from a network of generators, electricity had been wired through the lintels, along one side, a larger collection of wires- the telephone network- was opposite. When they had come for their first visit, it had been only a few men at a time. The potential danger of losing one of these hard built tunnels to enemy discovery was bad enough without risking a large number of attacking troops before it was absolutely necessary. The effect of this was now a deeper sense of enclosure, other bodies taking up the only space left between walls. Going so far underground, to the unfamiliar, eroded sense of direction and distance, even when travelling in a roughly straight line. A handy thing, then that direction forward was unmistakeable, the ground surged and shuddered with more intensity at the edge closest to the German lines; shock from each shell of the bombardment passed as a rolling tide, a heavy blast enough to cascade a chalk dust from the scrapes and flicker the delicate filaments. Unsettling as it was, it would be pithy to lament their situation too much. Twelve hours would be the most any would spend here, and the shelling was not addressed to them. Its intensity, still felt here, was severely diluted from what was being experienced under the fall of shot. None too many here, now, getting ready to fight, had any altruism available to pity those under the guns. The more Fritz suffered, the less they would, and they were more than happy with that arrangement.

From time to time along its length, 'Schlump Subway's walls gave way to alcoves. Some were abrupt, made large enough to house a generator or telephone relay. Others were proper galleries, stacked with munitions or supplies, or outfitted with cots which would soon be accepting the wounded. The subway let out into a spacious gallery, a hub, which fed into the individual saps. Each channel had been labelled with paint directly on the rock, a freehand codified with geometric shapes assigned to identify small units, a numerical designation matching that on the planning diagram and the nickname for the terminus. Six Platoon would be filing into the sap which led to the point they had come to know as 'Castle Switch Exit'. Not a single word had been breathed since they had come into 'Schlump Subway'. There was too much on individual minds to crowd the narrows with air vocalising them. Individual they may be, these musings broke down into three general categories. The minority of them, men of the 'old guard' were lost in what they had seen in battle before, having then been told how easy it was all going to be. They were hearing that again, and were reserving opinion a little more scrupulously than they had that first time. There was a larger third, made up of those who had come along between then and now. Having seen varying levels of this war as it played out from day to day, these men were seasoned, but ultimately untested in this extreme. Balance was made up of those who had only just come in, the reinforcements sent specifically for the upcoming battle. Of all the men here, it was these who really didn't know what they were in for. Every one of them, old to new and those middling used whatever memories they had, or filled an anxious blank in thinking the same singular thought:

"Am I going to die?" That they were spending this reflection in what could have not be a less tomb-like surrounding wasn't lost on many, no matter what group they fell into.

For Felix, this had been a continual process, part of which was the separating out of things not to be carried forward. The most recent letter from Ma was placed in the pile of all she had sent before, along with the less frequent post from his sister, and he supposed James would be adding to that. Felix's head shook involuntarily, James, in the RFC? This was the boy upon being told off to not put anything larger than his elbow in his lug hole had spent the afternoon trying to put his elbow in his lug hole, and someone had thought it a grand idea to let him at an aeroplane? Boxing clever, while he was at this, Felix had decided to empty his pockets of anything lacking a quality of possible usefulness in the next day or so. With the letters was put a number of pre-stencilled postcards, quick-fire mindings to send home, the soldier having struck out any of the supplied phrases that didn't reflect his situation. Felix had a couple of parody ones he'd clipped from trench newspapers. He'd not intended to mail these as his mother wouldn't have appreciated the joke. He'd send them to James. Underneath all those letters, he'd secreted his medal and course certificate, Battalion Transport having a share of dishonest men about. Amongst this went those lovely maps, the company and platoon aide memoirs Thorncliffe had Sweeny give out at orders the other day. If taken by Fritz, they'd provide no geographic news, but they did lay out these new tactics in a breathtakingly simple approach that the intelligence contained transcended language. Felix had had his fill of bloody maps and was glad to leave them behind. 'Flagstaff' and 'Pivot Stumps' were clearly visible; they could be seen by periscope from the trenches. They'd be much closer on the morrow. One map he would have was an intricate affair only of use for the first two hours of the attack. Solid black contour lines, evenly spaced delineated the lift and shift of the covering barrage, as far as, confusingly, a slightly thicker dark hash-the Black Line. No matter that, pleased he was his stop was the Red Line, without all that downhill fighting. Nearly neglected, as it had been pushed into the seam of a pocket, worn, and blurred, was the prayer to St Gertrude. He'd had it with him since February, since that night going out on a fool's errand, and as it seemed to have been working then, he kept it with him now. It was in French, anyway, and although Felix remembered the gist of it, the individual words meant little. Fancy a German trying to make sense of that, he pondered.

A scrap of creased yellow paper was next, this being the telegram the Padre had given him, quite purposeless now. Missus Pippin would be getting two of them. Leland had sought Felix out the other day. A patrol from Nine Platoon had found the body, Leland making the point that he'd only had three rounds left in his rifle.

"Who told him to do that?" Felix had demanded of the only other living witness of the failed bombing party.

"No one- it was him, insistent. We did what we could for Belfry; but me and Ferguson owe our lives to that wee man."

One last object puzzled him as he placed his hand upon it in his pocket. It was a button, and at first he thought it was one of his spares. Bringing it out and turning it over, it was the wrong shape and size to be of British issue, he remembered. That one raid, tumbling into the German trench, at first they found nothing, then according to plan, they'd fanned out to create the menace they had come for. Felix had bent down to examine a body laying still on the duckboards. His stance was such that when a rather animate corpse swung his legs against Felix's heels, it knocked the raider on his backside. At once the German was on top of him, straddled and pinning him, a meaty fist thrown downward caught his cheek, scraping the skin and knocking his head on the boards in recoil. The stars seemed a bit brighter. The second hit was worse, smashing into his temple, extinguishing the stars and much of everything else as a darkness clouded the corners of his vision. A third punch didn't land. A slickly coated steel blade burst forth from his assailant's chest, with that spatter of blood. The cut had shorn off a tunic button which had struck Felix's face in insult more than injury. Fern had withdrawn the knife, but the fellow hadn't been done in. The German turned, unbalanced, to face the man who'd just run him through. Ferguson wasted nothing of time and lunged forward- edge out- and cut the wind from him. Felix had been far too dizzy from the punches to have been much good the rest of that night. Although, to be fair, he'd at least had the rest of that night, and more besides. It may be he'd had to resign himself that he couldn't hold Ferguson accountable for Pippin, nothing had erased that uncertainty about Collier. The whole thing lacked an appropriate amount of sense.

Felix had cinched the straps on his pack close, dropping his weight down to himself and fighting equipment. Keeping the artillery schedule with a blank notepad and a stub of pencil wasn't going to slow him any or prevent room for a couple more Mills bombs or another bandolier. Bringing his worldly goods over to the Platoon pile, he'd collected his Section for the march forward.

Thorncliffe was no different than any of his men in thought, except the added dimension of command gave him so much more to consider. The question he needed to ask himself wasn't if he had told his men everything, or even to have told them enough. It was the question of if he had prepared them enough to be able to do the job without him. Junior officers, such as he, became casualties at a disproportionate rate than that of other ranks. Inspiration and decisiveness were best accomplished up front, where visibility was greatest for everybody, including the enemy. To that end, Thorncliffe had adopted a private's jacket and fighting equipment in place of his officer's tunic and Sam Browne belt. He'd kept his pistol, but would be armed much like the majority of his platoon with the Short Magazine Lee

Enfield. As his men all knew him at sight and the pitch of his voice, Thorncliffe needn't do anything by way of appearance to stand himself out. Sinclair and McCormack had both met him at the gallery where 'Schlump Subway' ended.

"Good luck, Patrick. I want you to know you were given this job for a reason," said the Colonel, "I know to expect good things from you."

"Won't let you down, Sir. These are the best damned men anyone could have to work with." Thorncliffe's reply was without pride or boastfulness. He so loved his platoon, his belief in its members was complete. Captain McCormack had said nothing at all, only appearing haggard and overtired. His burden was certainly no less than his platoon commanders, though for the first time they would be moving beyond his direct control. In another age, an officer in McCormack's position could rely on radio to remain in touch, the best the man could hope for was that his runners would outlast the day and the telephone back to Battalion remained serviceable without syphoning his linesmen. Captain McCormack's greatest concern was, what with this structure that had been adopted, he was out of his depth. Line command never being his ambition, operating at a distance from his platoons, and they from each other settled in a solitary feeling the plain dress he'd put on did nothing to hide; the remains of the bottle likewise failing to settle him.

Colonel Sinclair had not muted himself. His immediate command post was still in this underground, he and his staff would establish the new Advanced Headquarters on the best spot of ground resting in their hands by dinner-time tomorrow. Tomorrow being a big day, Sinclair wanted to look his best. A man of another age, he revelled in ceremony, the mystic nature of propriety and ritual standing at the foundation of all things martial. Mrs. Sinclair loved to go dancing with the dashing horseman, his sure steps a subconscious call of the beat which told the correct foot to plant; his pride in a good turnout turning her friend's jealous eyes.

All of these men, and so many thousands besides all had to reach terms with what may come in the next few hours. Many occupied themselves by marking the chalk, etching out their names, crude cartoons or tributes to the units they represented. It was best an effort at immortality as could be hoped for as much as it was distraction. Taverly was quite an artist and was well into a carving of the King's

Own regimental badge which Felix was admiring, turning away to a tap on his shoulder.

"Oh, it's you."

"I heard you talked to Leland," Ferguson said. It was the most either had spoken to the other in weeks, outside necessity of working together. Felix had no choice in that, as Thorncliffe didn't cede to his wish to have Ferguson removed. The Lieutenant had to explain the limited ability- as in none- Felix had in hiring or firing. Ferguson was good at his job and the two of them had been friends for ages. Thorncliffe wasn't interested in what may have come between them; a falling out over responsibility for young Pippin going West, perhaps, he just needed them to work together. For the rest of March, and this first week of April the barest minimum had been spoken between them.

"Who told you that?" Felix asked.

"Who do you think? Leland himself."

"So?" Felix realised that Taverly had stopped working on his art and was listening in. "Take a break, Tav. Somewhere else, like." Taverly moved along with difficulty.

"Somewhere else, you say? I'll just take the elevator to the penthouse then," he said in protest.

"So, you've heard about Squeak?" Felix only nodded. "Anything to add, Felix?"

"Alright. Leland says it happened same as you says it did. So I suppose that much is true."

"Why not go the whole way and take my word on everything else? How could I have known Pippin had seen it?"

"What, that Collier was about to kill you; he was some kind of lunatic?"

Ferguson shook his head. What Leland had said to him had been to be even with his friend. Like Thorncliffe, the man from Nine Platoon didn't concern himself with the business of a row between mates. He'd only come to confirm Pippin had been found.

"He wasn't about to kill me," he admitted, taking a further breath, "he thought he was about to kill you."

The pistol, being used sometimes as a device for emphasis as he illustrated his will with exaggerated sweeps of his hand, Collier had only briefly passed it with any concern to Ferguson's front.

"We'll be killed, Sir, all of us. We're only here to look for-" It was then the Colt was snapped tight on his frame.

"Wrong. The both of us <u>are</u> going to die, Strachan. Me, up there, you, down here, it doesn't matter. Did it matter to that man by the side of the road?"

"I'm not Strachan," Ferguson had suggested, but the other man may not have heard, as he had busied himself in recalling to pull the slide back on the automatic to chamber a round. Too dangerously deranged to be left to his own process, Ferguson ended him. It was a favour the victim had wished in any event, but to Hell with that if it were to involve anyone else going the same way.

Ferguson now had less of an idea as to what all of this meant than Felix had begun to discern. There had been something a little odd on first blush with Collier, but Felix had put that down as nerves. Perhaps there was to be an inquiry after all, and the feckless dolt had confused which man to take to the wire with Pippin and which to leave with the Lewis gun.

That February day had seen Collier appear at Captain Lafferty's desk. The young officer knew a surprising amount on the patrols planned for the evening. Could he take Six Platoon's party out? There were some details he needed for these maps of his. Consulting with Sinclair, the Adjutant had sent Collier off to find Sergeant Douglas and organise the patrol. When the Second Lieutenant turned the corner on to Upper Victoria Park, a shell went off, yards away but close as inches to the unprepared. He flinched terribly, dropping to a knee. As he looked up, the chap was watching him. Collier felt a recognition, said nothing and continued looking for the Sergeant. It wasn't seeing that man which bothered him as much as the memory of the other one that was there. Memory had frozen that moment, as the terrified expression of the man whose name he'd borrowed, face red, screaming,

"For the love of God, somebody help me!" The sight of him was what awaited the officer accountable when he tried to sleep each night since.

An apologetic palm was placed on Ferguson's shoulder. "Let's not worry about that now. Bigger things afoot. I'm going to have a peek." Felix moved off, through the sea of forms standing and sitting in whatever space could be found, to the sealed gate at the mouth of the tunnel, a fraction of lattice providing a post-box view of the war outside. He was taken aback at what he saw. Snow. At this time of year, of all things.

"They're catching Hell out there, eh, Catscratch?" It was Lieutenant Thorncliffe, and the two spent a few moments, remembering when; times so long ago but bright in the mind as the day before. Thorncliffe took out his watch.

"Oh, nuts! Fifteen minutes. Fifteen minutes!" A murmur of voices carried the message. "Six Platoon, by Section, in line." The men shifted themselves, forming two lines with backs to the cavern walls, in order of their departure.

"Remove breech covers." Done.

"Fix bayonets." Snap.

"Nelson, you in good puff this morning?"

"Braw, Sir. Well ye caw the tune?" Thorncliffe rubbed his chin in thought.

"We're at the front of Buckshee today. Company March is prudent." This just so happened to be Nelson's favourite, and he smiled wide.

"'Highland Laddie' it is, Sir."

"Good. Six Platoon! Forward on my signal. Dress off on your section commanders; section commanders dress off on Platoon HQ. Don't hang about, don't bunch up, don't stop for nothing. Good luck to you all." The final fifteen minutes, Lieutenant Thorncliffe spent inspecting the men one last time. A quick word, a nervous joke, each man, he found had a trembling handshake. Those with a taste for prayer were not inclined to keep the minutes remaining in idle and unaimed thoughts as the dawn eked a little brightness through the shedding clouds.

Chapter XXII

Zero Hour was just one more moment in an unstoppable addition of moments such as these. A small charge blew the gate outward, Thorncliffe was through before it all settled, Nelson a bit less game, not wanting the debris around his pipes. It was the officer's whistle alone the men heard in a single steady breath before Nelson could start wailing. Felix shook Bert's hand, he was standing across from him, before the both of them turned and followed Thorncliffe out into the open air. There didn't seem to be a lot of it. With the wind at their backs, the snow was driving right into the covering wall of shrapnel, now moving forward. Huge mines had and were being blown up and down the line, throwing their lot with the bombardment still seeking targets. Thorncliffe was waving Felix forward, and with only a slight glance behind, he stepped off quick, One Section in two line on his heels. As they kicked past, Sergeant Douglas moved in line with the last man, Ferguson, followed next at a cautious interval by

Thorncliffe and his team, flanked by Three and Two Sections, Tapscott and his Lewis gun boys forming the base of the square that was a platoon in Artillery Formation. Loosed rifle grenades tumbled toward that hated apex of the German line. Both casements had suffered plenty already, their concrete stressed and chipped. MG Number One was missing a corner, rusted bars the skeletal remains. Sutherland's contribution was more an effort at keeping Fritz' head down than adding to structural collapse. They didn't even add much to the sound of it all, just subtle coughs of the blank cartridges which propelled the grenades. Four uneven bursts clotted about the switch, exactly as they should have, at the same time Felix reached 'Flagstaff.' Nary so much as a whisper had been heard from the German trench yet. They moved with what speed they could, ultimately checked by the wall of shrapnel walking the ground before them, bursting with timed fuses, at ten feet from the ground, or with graze fuses, upward upon contact with the earth. Regardless of direction, each one was an oversized shotgun blast, arcing heavy lead bearings in a wide spread. During rehearsals, staff officers with bright white armbands stood in place of the barrage, moving at a timed pace over the ersatz ridge. The most that would happen if in this practice, Felix brought up his men too quickly, would be a tongue-lashing reflecting his intelligence, ancestry and future reproductive prospects. Bad as that may have been, pride recovered faster than a body might under a close brush on the day.

Artillery Formation, this streamlined box they had shifted into which kept their frontage compact during the initial step-off reduced the immediate target they presented also allowed them a short distance to acclimatize with everything happening up ahead. Felix saw his mark nearly straight off. Besides having clocked it with the periscope yesterday, it was right where it had been on the maps burned into his mind and the final preparations on the mock-up. The shallow ground from which they exited was the only serious impediment to having eyes on. Plus, with all this whirring and crashing about, there was plenty to distract a mind prone to wandering. Lieutenant Thorncliffe had made this first maker unmistakable, and inspiringly rallying. As Felix had to know what to look for, he'd been ruined of the surprise, told to keep it to himself with a wink from the sly young officer. 'Flagstaff' for want of something suitable, was Thorncliffe's ash cane- he'd gone out Saturday night to plant it himself. There it stood, having sunk a bit as mud gathered and receded in its own temperate tide, to a more abject angle than upright. As his hands were to be full of rifle today, Thorncliffe could spare the cane, an item more of swagger or status than fighting quality. His final touch had been knotting a yard length of the Regimental tartan around the crook. Soaked, its colours appeared blended, muted. The wind, sharply passing through lifted the swatch in short waves, a pennant pointing them towards danger, step by step as it was. Felix put his whistle to his lips. Goodness, it was cold. One solid heave on it cut a note that ran right over Nelson hitting the bridge on the march. He flung his arms out, parallel as he could make them to ground moving gently, then sharply, to higher points. This position Felix held only for an instant, only enough for the next man to see and begin the transition from first positions to second. Just so there was no mistake, he also called out, as he'd been told, "Flagstaff! Flagstaff!" Even though he'd been warned off not stopping for anything, Felix estimated they were all making rather good time anyway, and shaved a second off the day to re-plant the cane a touch more straight, and moved sharply along, the men of his section unfolding, Felix the fulcrum, to re-form abreast.

The call sounded back through the ranks of Six Platoon, at first, plainly as "Flagstaff", but quickly added as afterthought by those first past the post, seeing it for the first time, "it's the Sir's stick!" Some men whooped or let out a restrained cheer, such a thing enough to steel them further for the terrible work ahead. Nestled as it had been in Artillery Formation, Six Platoon, from the effect of constant drills, cantered out into a slightly echeloned outstretched line of sections. Sutherland's grenadiers were fixing up for the second volley, working another blank into the breach and bombs over the muzzle cap, while moving into Attack Formation. The Platoon's next waypoint was a bit more obvious to all involved, a hump of shattered trees many had clamoured over or past if out on patrol in this neighbourhood. Men of experience knew the lay of this land, those without stuck relying on a realisation of familiarity with the training ground, after a fashion. No longer a lone stand of robust trees, the feature now christened "Pivot Stumps" stood with little defiance or beauty left. Thick bases of what still rooted of old trunks would accept Four Section in its obscuring folds. Tapscott was charging towards that, in relativity to the shrapnel moving, measuredly, farther off; his section equally determined to reach it. Atherton pumped his empty arm in a trot while his other balanced the Lewis across a shoulder at the slope. For these terse two minutes in the getting there, since the heavy Lewis was more effective moved into a stable position than being fired from the hip, Atherton had yet to provide any offensive input. Eager for this, on finally making the distance over an agonising buck-twenty worth of seconds, the gun was swung out from its travelling position, his off-hand striking the barrel shroud, popping the feet of the bipod out and locked. He melted forward, his first reply a rattling burst struck his point of aim before he really settled in to work. In between shots of opportunity, in tandem with the Lewis, the rest of Four Section passed along the first portion of spare drums to Robbins. Atherton was singular; a shift up or down, just a nudge, a slight windage, another burst. The same movement, again and again, with variations according to his judgement, or Robbins flagging his attention to possible targets. Atherton tried to keep on top of this rather than get his cues from the number two gunner. This wasn't so much a feeling of wishing to be superior, but the accepted method for Robbins to gain his attention was to slap the back of his helmet. Robbins had a streak of excitability about him and this was transmuted into unintentionally jarring strikes over Atherton's skull. This could be forgiven as the lad was sharp on the reload. In a blink, from the 'clunk' of a bare chamber, the next pan was in as fast as a sweatshop boy could replace a bobbin, which was how Robbins came to this skill, and the gun could immediately continue its stitching.

Thorncliffe and Platoon HQ were close in behind and set up to control the attack from this point, where the Lewis would shortly be accompanied by rifle grenades, thus becoming the base of fire. From the biggest guns on offer, re-purposed naval pieces, crushing their quarry downrange several hundredweight at a time, through the mix and match of heavy, medium and field guns, all contributed in a process now in its second week of "winning the firefight." Whittled down as the battle became a series of specifics rather than one generality, it was now to Six Platoon's base of fire; the Lewis, the rifle bombs and a baker's dozen of that workhorse, the Lee Enfield to conclude it, allowing One and Two Sections to slink out on either side of 'Pivot Stumps' on their approach for the envelopment. Another symphony of anticlimactic coughs told of Three Section's second sending aloft. The Lieutenant looked to his left, and his right, a glance at first, snapping an assessment of things so far, planting his eyes more firmly on any detected trouble spots. Only a light shuffle had been needed to get this far, the lip of 'Castle Switch Exit' a spit away, so it was his animated heart, not physical effort that stripped his wind. Nelson had quit playing, having gone a full round on 'Highland Laddie.' Thorncliffe told him to save up breath and keep his pipes safe, it would be the Regimental March when next they advanced, as soon as those signal flares from the assaulting sections, pray, both, landed. Everything, everything, everything had gone just about right so far, he thought, from a mind unfamiliar with what not to say about scoreless games until they're done. Not a man down, from his point of view, weapons in full action and Sergeant Douglas moving in to tie up between One and Three Section, where he'd remain in place with the latter, at a good point to monitor the former's assault. He stumbled a bit over rutted ground, but made the trek with little bother. Sergeant Douglas' word would be the last bit of overhead for Felix, from that the young corporal would be cut loose to take his men the final yardage.

Distantly, there was that great heap, way off to the north. Hill Such-and-Such, Thorncliffe had forgotten the numbers, it was well outside his patch. It loomed over all else as the highest feature of a high feature. Thorncliffe couldn't see all the way to it in a straight line, the rise of terrain here keeping only a portion of its crest visible. Shiny with wire and ringed with shrapnel it was going to be sheer murder to the boys going up that- another Highland regiment, from the West Coast and Prairies, he'd been told, so that comforted Thorncliffe that they wouldn't let the side down. A bright flash, then two more at first dazzled him, but quickly pointed to where he should have been looking. Splinters of wood and steel, encouraged by the charge of those potato mashers Fritz could throw, pin-like a heaving great distance jigged about the stumps of the old copse. A second sequence touched off, thick dirt and those heavenly torn trees absorbing much of it, though the cheering of earlier, that eternity of a handful of minutes prior had been replaced by isolated howls. Thorncliffe's sleeve was torn searing heat peeling through skin drenching itself. The tin hat received a number of bumps and his cheek gouged far worse than a clumsy barber would have his two bits rescinded for.

"Where is that coming from?" He demanded of anyone, himself especially; he was in charge here, after all. Out of place, in colour and contour, a line of steel tortoise filed along a ditch, of fresh earth, leading, it was so fucking clear, even in the snow, from a fold behind a breech in the German wire all the way down to what had been assured was an abandoned observation post.

"Shift fire!" He shouted. "Tap- watch to your right, Three Section, two up on that OP!" The Lewis replied, thankfully, along with solitary rifle shots, mixed now with things travelling just as hostile in the opposite direction. Sutherland had tagged two grenadiers, who immediately snap-shot the German's hasty approach. Three's other pair of bombers plunged fire onto the machine gun casements continually, which still had done nothing. Their apertures were too narrow and dark to even tell if the guns were mounted. Thorncliffe pulled a bomb from his pocket, intending to add it to suppressing those chancy bastards pouring out from that OP, but the tear in his arm was bad enough to reconsider his ability to make a good toss. An aggravated slice of dismembered moments followed of ragtime as arranged for the .303, steady bursts from the Lewis, an aria of 7.92 and bombs of all sorts of design; flurried one way, the next.

Advantage of ambush lost, Fritz beat back to his line, prudence not a quality assigned only to their enemy. They'd be contained and cut down if they stayed, so they would stop the oncoming assault from their own wire; counterattacks from the reverse slope would push the enemy back; one German Platoon NCO telling his men: "*Wir werden sie gehen und klopfen sie mit einem Besen thiss Hügel von uns wie eine Frau aus Mäuse aus ihrer Küche jagen[1].*" Crashing into an enemy advance as they had done was not at all to be anything but a spoiling blow, to put them on their back feet, slow them down, separate the *Kanadianer* from that shield of lead bearings. Sufficient time, *Bitte Gott*, to have those machine guns brought out from protective cover and start peeling these *schweinn* from their works.

It had been called the race for the parapet, this sprint, though Thorncliffe realised it was more properly a steeplechase; up this, through that, over the next. Severe penalties could be had for missing a gate, and both factions in this scrap were at the same game of incurring those penalties. Nelson was by his side, where had Sweeny gone? The piper was trying to tie down a field dressing on the Lieutenant's

---

[1] "We will stop them here and knock them off this hill as an old woman would chase mice from her kitchen with a broom."

arm while the officer was on the move closer to his gun crew. As he would before crossing a busy street, he looked again to right and left, seeing now his vanguard had made their final points, the fuss here just now of little bother to them and as they were meant to, carried themselves forward without too much as a sideways glace, except to the thirst of curiosity. Thorncliffe spat, blood and shattered teeth, it appeared his cheek had been ripped right through, the splinter's inertia spent against more than a few molars. With his good hand, he pulled his Very gun loose, already loaded with a green signal flare. He sent it free, and its light passed through the snow in an effect of great spectacle, a dancing lively corona reflected, oh so minutely, by tumbling crystals of frosty water. Looks were one thing, and a sight as marvellous is bound to find place in the catalogue of the mind belonging to those at witness, its existence was beyond the unexpected aesthetic conditions created. This was the signal for the assault.

Spread now at the furthest distance from the rest of the platoon, seeing the flare was a relief, it unbridled the two attacking sections. There was no need to have any of the maps Felix had not been allowed to bring. He was intimately familiar with where he was about to lead his men. Fritz did not have a stereotype to being exacting without a fair amount of evidence. It was so perfectly constructed, so visually fooling that this exit, to its maker's understanding, had never been properly discovered by those probes over the winter. Had anyone known, it would have been closed off. Leaving the OP, despite that loss weeks ago was a gamble, certainly, a ruse of war. Circumstances had kept the false assurance the Germans had that the cunning exit here had kept its secret. Once there had been a raid planned here, events along this ground had forced it being called off, and it was never remounted. The innovative way the gaps in the wire had been hidden from plain sight meant that it was in a blind spot from the casements. Ideally, the machine guns would have forbidden any encroachment. Confusion over the bombardment shifting made for an ill-timed hesitation and the hard points remained silent and still the focus of Sutherland's industrial archers. At the front of his section, Felix reached the forward edge of wire, much scattered and torn in snapped lengths from bent and crumpled pickets, thanks to men like Billy and his mates. High explosive had raked the area, picking the iron floss apart in great bunches. In a slight variance from Thorncliffe's plan, because Felix knew it was here, he'd been allowed to make a probe at the sally port. If it was still open, One Section could crest the trench and penetrate towards their goal with a great deal more speed. This chosen causeway forced One Section to approach in two waves, four wide. Felix, slightly ahead of the first team saw the Mills bombs hey had chucked go overhead and disappear up the hill and into the trench and moved forward tenderly, but swiftly, reaching the half-way point as they went off. The rear rank, under Ferguson, took that as their go-ahead to add their bombs. A further succession of heavy thuds and crushed air kept within the confines of the German fie bay reverberated and were pushed furiously upward. Cascaded over the trench, the charcoal mist of fragments and dirt were added to by bits of wood, jagged and just as vicious, rags and flesh. The ground pulsed underneath One Section, coming up the slope at a full run, bayonets at the point, it was a fair bit steeper than it had been in practice. At the top, spilled sandbags gathered loosely about the detritus of cumulative artillery and the grenades freshly detonated. It scattered Felix's feet and took him slightly off level, and in a bound he vaulted the parapet, landing below in a scrabble. To his right, the traverse was right where it was meant to be, as it had been on those endless up-the-hill, down-the-hill days last month, now in three very real dimensions. Sutherland's grenades were still thumping the bunkers up ahead, beyond this first blind corner. Felix first team were coming over the bags as he went for the traverse. Just at the turn, his ears ringing with noise and the rush of blood which felt his thoughts were pulsing with each heartbeat, there, inches past his eyes a gleam of metal took longer to process in mind than his body did in springing to parry. The crack of wood on wood shocked through Felix's hands, but he held firm. Supplemented by repetitive drill, instinct; that deep level of such an impulse shared across all living things, that singular will took command. Before the next blow could be delivered, with his opponent's point swept down, guard open, Felix drew his arms back, taught, stepped one pace forward-the drill returning to help. "Every movement in bayonet fighting is followed by ONCE PACE FORWARD!" Old RSM Knox had showed them how it was done. Release, quick, straight ahead, cant the weapon to the right, and purchase; the blade disappearing into the Fieldgrau in front of him, which darkened with a spreading blotch. The man curled, doubled up over the steel, feet lifted by Felix's rush. Felix surprised himself that he was screaming, like a wild man, a savage. Lowering his rifle, he smashed his boot against the German, pulling the weapon free. The man collapsed where he was, his hands futily trying to stop life from parting. Sloane, Tremaine, Edmund and Plumrose in turn leapt over the wretched shape to rush the bunker, bombs ready. Considering this one at his feet was out of being a threat, Felix set to follow his men. Before he could, Fritz tried in one last gasp to get up; again that will to live which can supersede even common sense urged to be obeyed. This failed, and he crashed to the trench floor, on his back, legs folded under, gory, gurgling pink bubbles pushed between his lips. Twisted in agony, the face was unmistakable. Ulrich. He still had Osgoode's pistol tucked into his wide leather belt. The men who'd overtaken Felix while he was engaged with him had flushed the machine gun post, and were sorting out a bag of prisoners, grey; head to foot, in uniform and the dust of minced concrete. More than a few were bloody; all were sullen. Sloane and Plumrose had rifles trained down the communication trench holding this point for the following wave, Edmund and Tremaine corralled the prisoners, all that remained was for one of Bert's fellows tying in here. Felix came about to retrace the trench and check his second team, who were to be holding a bay and the first traverse to the left of where they'd all come in. A footstep towards that locale was halted by the blasting echo of powerful, rapid shots concussing the lateral walls. It was a frenzy ending as abruptly as it began, nothing followed; Felix rushed the corner. Immediately apparent was that Ulrich did indeed have some fight left in him. O'Leary had taken a pistol shot at such close range as to dispatch him completely, his solid frame enough to further wreck the foot planks where he'd landed with full force. Ulrich was quite all the way dead now, too, as he'd collected a bullet himself, directly above the rough gape of where Felix had torn into him. He'd managed to crawl to a corner, propping himself, almost sitting upright, no doubt catching the Bulldog looking the other way. The .45 had tumbled from still hands, landing by his tall boots, slide locked back, empty. A fractional moment occurred where Felix couldn't help to admire this resilience, managing to get his last word in before the end. O'Leary accounted for one slug, so when Felix turned towards the trench front, he could sum up the remainder. Some sandbags along the parapet had taken a further pasting, Ferguson had interrupted a couple on their way to the wall, and they had knocked a good deal of him with them as they went.

"Andy!" The man was a mess. He'd come to rest on the firestep, looking quite comfortable, most of his vitality splattered about the rough bags and wooden revetments. In that mercy which can sometimes happen, while still somehow alive, what remained of function was busily trying to sort itself out and Ferguson was dreamily unaware of the present. He put his head back, skyward, his helmet a cradle as he relaxed against the trench. A distant, glazed look had washed over his eyes. Felix had seen this look before, this confusion of a man going past a transition he would not be around to illustrate.

"Andy," Felix called again, more gently, shock having a brief shelf life when each moment here was a different variety of shock.

"I think I'm ill, Felix. Do I have to go on parade?"

Felix sat next to him, embraced his friend's shoulder with one arm.

"No, you're excused. We'll have Salinger take a look at ye."

"Thanks."

"I want you to know you did the right thing. Andy, d'ye hear me, you did the right thing." He was gone.

The dead could look after themselves for the time being; Felix needed to finish what had started; check in with Tav and Brent that Five Platoon had made the meeting. Tav he met coming the other way.

"Jesus, Tav, stay with Brent."

"Coming to tell you Five's up. Brent's fine. What happened here?" Felix hustled him back.

"We're down a couple, get yerself back to where you belong, nosy bastard." He turned back to the grim scene of the fire bay. Mills bombs had spilled earth by way of the shelling having ruined the revetting. An assortment of aged remains, of men caught for lack of grace by the artillery, left unburied for safety's sake by others sheltering nearby over a fortnight hence. They had been alternately buried and disinterred one explosion at a time. Gaining entry by Mills bombs added a few, those who had been getting ready to repulse their enemy. The freshest trio held a voluminous tableau, a strict lesson of what men could still do to each other after tonnes of iron and fire had been dropped from above, choking clouds searing the lungs, that at this point it became intensely personal in an impersonal way. Every ounce of suffering taken first hand, witnessed or even heard about could, on these rare occasions of going toe to toe, be focussed on something as equally fragile and fallible, be expressed as a rage for which elsewhere other than this nightmare there could be no excuse. This was why, despite the better of a fair to middling sense of propriety, sticking a man, regardless of who he was, presented as a relieving fantastic sensation. Never to be breathed, ever, Felix decided right then, was how much he'd enjoyed it.

"Catscratch!" Tremor was calling him.

"Yeah?"

"We're with Bert. All good." Felix said nothing. "Are you alright?"

Felix waved towards the mess between them.

"Aw, damn bad luck. Feel foolish for wanting to complain about the noise."

"We'll lay 'em down, cut their kilt aprons and keep the outside off of them. Not now. Get over to Brent and Tav, they need a spare body. We're going to start the strongpoint over by the MG."

"Sure thing." The redoubt they were to build was to have been at this place, if it had not been reduced and repurposed into an open air ossuary. Over by the bunkers would have to do. Felix couldn't take any more reflective moments and needed to see if Bert had things in hand, firing the pen light that broadcast success as he went.

The barrage still held tight to these first hard-won points. The German line had been thoroughly pierced, thus enabling the second wave the opportunity to filter through and carry the rest of the day to the Black Line. Through that continuing racket, Felix could just pick up the warbling of Nelson playing forward, 'Cock o' the North', meaning Thorncliffe would be along shortly.

When he did show, the officer was slightly spoiled for a night out, having picked up a slight whistle through his cheek and his arm refused impulse to move. The rifle had been passed off, his pistol the easier choice now.

"How'd you do, Catscratch?"

"Two out. O'Leary, Ferguson. You staying up, Sir?"

"No withdrawal without orders, don't stop for the wounded."

"That's a wee bit literal." Thorncliffe tried to shrug.

"Wouldn't rather be anywhere else. We'll put the Lewis up here with your lot, and I'll see about sending a couple of files your way. Not sure what we've come up the hill with, they, well, this happened," he pointed to his injuries by way of explanation. Felix understood, Thorncliffe checked the time. "About twenty minutes to the next shift." This stunned Felix; had only that much time gone by- a quarter hour or a shade more? "Get the bags here as high as you can, let Atherton pick his ground when he gets here. Good stuff so far, let's keep our eyes forward."

Felix had no desire, in fact a total vacancy, for wanting to look behind.